M

a
Red Lion

Siobhán Carew

DuBois Publishing
Cambridge

First published in Great Britain 2025

Published by DuBois Publishing 2025

ISBN: 978-1-913410-22-3

Cover design: DuBois Publishing © 2025
cover photo: © Siobhán Carew
The Oak Room, The Red Lion, Soham, Cambridgeshire

First edition 2025

DuBois
publishing

www.duboispublishing.com

Dedicated to the memory of Peter Leonard

My dear friend, Peter Leonard, would have absolutely loved to be around to read this book. He would have thought it such fun and would have probably relished being portrayed as an evil landlord pantomime villain or some such.

Peter was the driving force behind The Red Lion, which he bought in 2015. He worked tirelessly to restore the building to its current glory after it had been left to decay slowly following decades of neglect.

Gas fires were ripped out to expose Victorian ones, which in turn were removed to reveal huge inglenooks. Lino was removed to be replaced by Cambridge Pamments*, painstakingly restored by Peter.

Damp was rife throughout the building and Peter was forced to use his ingenuity to come up with solutions. The bar was clad in recycled boards from barns, creating a wonderfully unique interior which is commented on frequently. The Victorian Room was panelled with decorative vents allowing the walls to breath.

Most people would have walked away from the Red Lion, as problems arose at a ferocious rate: the damp, the thatch, the famous gable end being held up by the phone box, the garden permanently under water. But Peter found solutions for all; cladding was erected, willow trees were planted, inglenooks were hastily bricked up to save the gable end. His vision never faltered and he remained chipper throughout.

I'm sure that if Peter were alive today he would have taken great pleasure in reading this novel, and will no doubt be raising a glass, from up high, to its publication.

Here's to you Peter!

Lucy Harper

*Floor tiles made of Cambridgeshire Gault clay

RED LION

RESTAURANT & BAR

SINCE 1620

Christmas Party Menu

Celeriac and Stilton soup with crème fraîche and chives
Crevettes with homemade dill mayonnaise (£4 supplement)
Smoked salmon pâté with dill and pink peppercorns
Salad of Neal's Yard goat's cheese with walnuts and quince
Pulled pork and mojo verde on Grain Culture sourdough
Pickled herrings with yoghurt and cucumber
Caponata on Grain Culture sourdough with black olives

Roast Suffolk Turkey with Newmarket pigs in blankets and chestnut stuffing
Beef Wellington with port gravy (£12 supplement)
Suffolk venison braised in port with wild mushrooms
Lebanese lamb with tzatziki and pomegranate
Fish of the day with crayfish saffron and cream
Slow roast belly of Blythburgh pork with crackling
Spinach pepper and ricotta roulade with pine nuts and a tomato and basil sauce

Christmas pudding with brandy cream
Chocolate almond and olive oil torte with caramel and crème fraîche
Coffee and amaretto semi freddo
Spiced apple and almond crumble
Raspberry and vanilla crème brûlée
Clementine and Grand Marnier trifle with almonds

Neal's Yard cheeses with homemade chutney (£4 supplement)

Mince pies and clementines

Coffee

2 Courses £32.00
3 Courses £40.00
4 Courses £50.00
(4th course is cheese)

A discretionary service charge of 10% will be added to your bill
If you would like any advice on allergens please ask a member of staff

17 HIGH STREET, SOHAM, CAMBRIDGE CB7 5HA   TEL: 01353 771 633
info@theredlionsoham.co.uk | instagram: red_lion_soham | www.redlionsoham.com

Harry's ragged table plan with notes

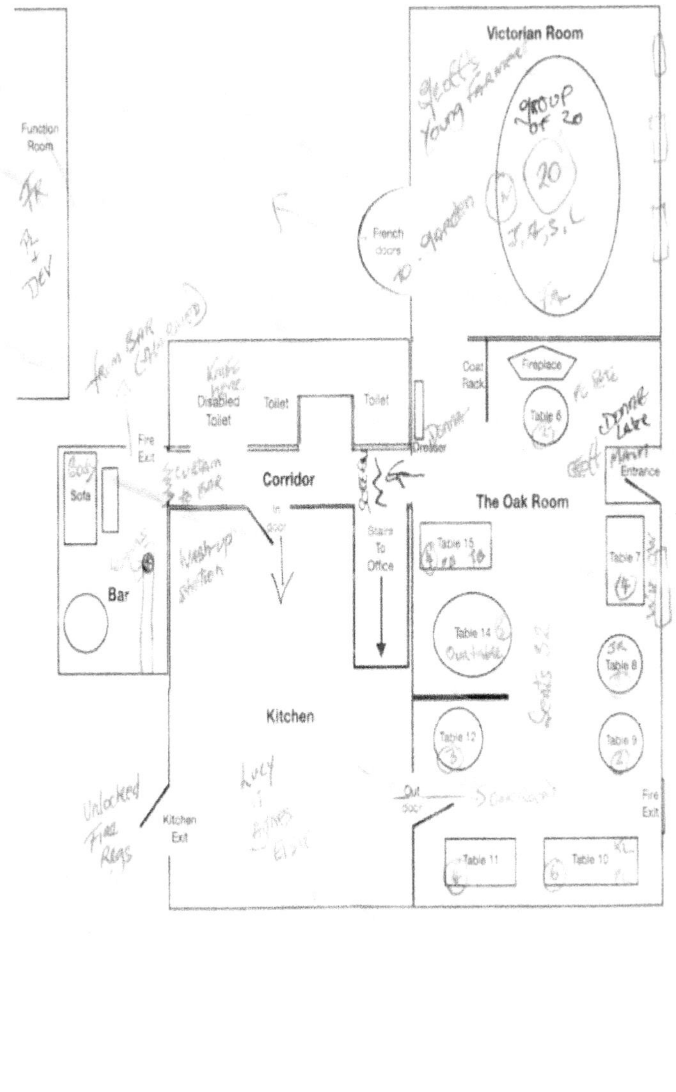

1

Harry Meredith's phone rang. The screen flashed *DCI Fountain Cambs Police.*

He swiped to accept the call. 'Good morning Ma'am.'

'How are you today, Harry?'

'I'm well.'

'Has your arm healed?'

'Nearly there, I'll soon be playing tennis again.'

'Hmm, getting stabbed is nasty. Torn muscle, tendon and ligaments take a long time to heal. You were lucky not to have nerve damage. It was foolish to wade in when you weren't wearing slash-resistant clothing.'

Harry flexed his arm. It was still a bit weak, and lifting weights was not something he would manage for a while, but… 'The man's wife was in danger, Ma'am, I couldn't just stand by.'

'Hmm.'

Harry knew that behind the tough front, the DCI was genuinely concerned. 'I can still work and be productive. My brain is fine,' he said, 'and since being a detective is often down to analysis and problem-solving, there's no reason for me to continue on sick leave.'

'As long as you don't overdo the physical side.'

'I won't Ma'am. Occupational Health has pronounced me fit to resume work and I shall return on Monday.'

'Good. Pop your head around my door and say hello. That aside Harry, Hugues Dubois is finishing his visit to Cambridge this week. I've organised a dinner at St Benedict's, but I thought his colleagues might take him out somewhere local. It would be a nice contrast to the formal college setting.'

Harry liked Hugues, or Oog, as he'd come to be called, but the man wasn't generally popular. Before Harry had been put on sick leave, he'd tried to set up a leaving outing for Oog but only Bradley, Harry's detective sergeant, had agreed to join in. He cleared his throat.

'Is there a problem, Harry?'

It was better not to say that while Harry had been off work, Oog had organised the evening out. Fortunately he had stuck with Harry's choice of venue.

'Are you still there, Harry?'

'Yes yes. Everything is fine. We're taking Oog to the Red Lion in Soham.'

'Is that a pub?'

'No, a restaurant.'

'In Soham? Is the food good?'

'Very.'

'Excellent.' DCI Fountain ended the call.

* * * * *

Harry went for a walk. The cold was refreshing. He walked towards the River Cam, along the side of the river which housed many of the colleges' boat clubs. He would miss these morning rambles once he was back at work.

Harry had rowed once, in his student days. How wonderful and free it had felt. He kicked at stones scattered along the path. Rowing was out of the question now. He stood a while to look on the river. It flowed quietly. There was hardly a ripple on the surface of the water. The stillness reminded him of his life, which, at present was static and dull. Especially his personal life. Time off work recovering had given him space to think. He had few regrets in his life, but of those few, the biggest was breaking up with Sara.

It was a year since they'd gone their separate ways. How could he have treated her so badly? And what might he do to mend the breach between them? In some respects he couldn't wait to be back at work, where he would be far too busy to ruminate.

A dog running so close that it brushed Harry's legs, jolted him out of his reflections.

'Sorry,' called the dog's owner, running slowly after it.

Harry smiled and shrugged. He liked dogs, liked them more than cats. Sara had a cat, a grumpy cat. But Harry would suffer Arabella gladly if it meant he could be with Sara again.

* * * * *

Lucy Harper and Donna Hobbs were in the kitchen of the Red Lion restaurant in Soham, preparing for the evening's customers. Donna held the list of bookings and was checking through it with a pen.

'The ex-Young Farmers are in the Victorian Room, as usual. That's Geoff Norman's group. He likes the Carmel Road red wine so I'll mention that to Agnes.' Donna scribbled a note next to the booking. 'Have we checked final numbers and meals with him?'

'Yes,' said Lucy, 'I phoned him last week. There are twenty in the group. Beef Wellington is popular with them.'

'It's Geoff's favourite.' Donna worked further through her list. 'Oh, Harry Meredith. We haven't seen much of him lately. I bet he'll order the beef too.'

'I didn't see his name on the list.'

'He didn't make the booking. Someone else called… Oog? Strange name. Anyway this Oog phoned, said he was a friend of Harry's. They'll be group of five. I've put them on table 14.'

'I must check how many servings of the beef we have.' Lucy opened the fridge and peered inside. 'Most of the diners are likely to choose turkey. I'll set three beef aside for Harry's table, add the four booked for the not-so-Young Farmers.'

Donna chuckled. 'Maybe we should call them the Beef Wellington Appreciation Society.'

Lucy laughed. 'Yes! That leaves five more servings. We must let Agnes and Elsie know. They should be ready to suggest alternatives when the beef is gone.'

'Okay. Oh, hang on Lucy, Tom Black phoned to book a table. He's also a fan of the beef. I've been able to squeeze him in because Table 15 are eating early before going on to something in Ely.'

'So not Tom's usual table?'

Donna shook her head. 'No. I've explained that to him.'

The door from the corridor opened. Clinking sounds of tables being laid with cutlery and glassware seeped through the gap.

A tall, well-built young woman, with light brown frizzy hair tied back in a ponytail, came in from the bar corridor. She was carrying an empty tray. 'Elsie is asking where the napkins are… again!'

'Give her a chance, Agnes. She only works weekends

and hasn't been here that long.'

'You're too soft, Donna. Elsie needs to get with the program.' Agnes laid her tray on a worktop and began filling it with water glasses. 'My cousin and his wife, Paul and Kylie, will be here this evening. Are they on the bookings list?'

'The Leonards? Yes.'

'Paul messaged me. They want a good table. They'll have that annoying Mrs Manners with them. Well, his wife is meeting her. Huh. Kylie is *so* ambitious. She wants to open her own hair salon and Paul said she's sucking up to Mrs Manners just because the woman is a district councillor. Paul says Kylie wants to get a use change, or something like that.'

'Right.' Donna didn't comment. She was used to Agnes's long explanations. 'They'll be sitting at one of the end tables in the Oak Room. Table 10 on the window side.'

Agnes stopped filling the tray. 'Couldn't Elsie serve in the Victorian Room this evening?'

Donna looked at Lucy. A tiny smile lifted the corner of Lucy's mouth. They were used to Agnes trying to order events the way she'd prefer them to be.

'I'd like to say hello to Paul. He's my cousin. The oldies won't notice if Elsie is a bit slow and you have their orders anyway.'

'I prefer that you work the Victorian Room,' said Donna. 'The wine and drink orders can be complicated. You're much better at that.'

Agnes grumbled as she finished filling her tray, then headed back to the main restaurant room through a second door in a corner of the kitchen. She was halfway through the door when she reversed rapidly. A couple of glasses fell off the tray and smashed onto the floor.

'Elsie!' she screamed. 'This is the 'Out' door! If you want to come *into* the kitchen, you need to use the 'In' door from the corridor! Like how many times have you been told that?'

'Sorry. I forgot.' Elsie leaned down to pick up the broken glass.

'Stop, you'll cut yourself,' called Donna. 'I'll get the brush and pan. Don't worry about it, Elsie. Accidents happen and things break. It's just the way it is, and you don't have to worry. Okay?'

Agnes tramped out of the kitchen with the remaining glasses. Elsie stood in the open doorway, her head hanging. Donna began sweeping up the glass fragments. Lucy and her sous-chef, Vi, carried on with food prep for the evening.

2

Harry pulled up Sara's number. He stared at it for a long time. Would she pick up if he phoned? He couldn't be sure. It was so totally his fault that they were no longer together. His affair with Maria had been brief but it had left a trail of destruction in its wake.

Clouds replaced the morning sun.

His neighbour's cat scratched at the window of the French doors. Harry didn't have the energy to shoo the animal away.

His phoned locked itself as Harry sat, undecided.

What would Sara think of his excuse to ask her out? Technically, it wasn't asking her out because he was simply inviting her to join a small group who were having a farewell dinner for Oog. She knew Oog because they were both at St Benedict's College in Cambridge. Would that make a difference?

Get a grip!

Harry unlocked the phone, hit Sara's number.

She answered on the second ring. That was a good sign. After asking how she was and even asking after her weird cat, Harry harrumphed to clear a frog in his throat, 'I'm organising a leaving dinner for Hugues Dubois–'

'For Oog?'

'Yes.'

'We call him Oog at college.'

'I know. The guys at the station do as well.'

'Hardly surprising. It's an impossible name to pronounce if you don't speak French.'

'Yeah. Well anyway I've booked dinner at the Red Lion in Soham on Saturday, 7th December. It should be a nice English treat before Oog returns to Paris. Will you join us, Sara?'

There was a long silence. He could hear her breathing so he knew she was still on the line.

'Please come, Sara. Please?' Damn, he hadn't meant to plead. She would think him pathetic. 'The food is scrumptious,' he mumbled.

Sara sighed. 'Dinner with you and Oog? He mentioned the other day that something was planned. He emails me a lot.'

'He emails you?'

'He has no choice,' she laughed. 'I won't give him my mobile number.'

Harry laughed too. Sara was no pushover. 'Good for you,' he said.

'Is asking me along Oog's idea?'

Harry stopped himself from pretending it had been Oog's idea. 'You're partly right. We're going to the Red Lion for a leaving meal and yes, he made a point of asking if you would be joining us. He has somehow managed to learn that you and I are… were, eh, friends.'

It was true that Oog had specifically asked if Sara would be one of the group. It was also true that Harry had been concerned to learn that Sara and the Frenchman had met frequently at their college. Oog had rattled on about her, likening Sara to the Botticelli Venus and raving about the way the candlelight in St Benedict's College dining hall had sparked lights in her golden hair.

Well Sara wasn't like a Botticelli Venus. The woman in that painting was, well, stout, and Sara was slim. That woman's hair flowed because she was on a shell at the edge of the sea. Sara was very much on land, and her hair was *red* gold and there was a curl in it, and sometimes it fluffed out and that was why it caught the light. If Sara was like any portrait, she might be Rossetti's Proserpine, his last version, where her hair is just like Sara's, and her eyes are sad.

It was mostly Harry's fault that Sara's eyes were sad. He wanted to put that right, wipe the sadness away – if he could, if she would agree to give him a second chance.

'I, ah, em–' muttered Sara.

'It's Oog's last outing before he returns to France. I suggested to the work crew that we make a fuss of him, take him somewhere nice to round off his stay in Cambridge, but, well… Bradley is the only one who has agreed to join us.'

Harry imagined Sara shaking her head. She used to smile at him, call him a softie, and in those moments she would struggle to say no to him. Ironic that he was using Oog to persuade her.

The twinge of jealousy Harry had initially felt on learning Sara and Oog knew each other had mostly passed. Oog simply wasn't Sara's type. But his admiration of her had given Harry the idea of combining his hitherto fruitless pursuit of Sara with taking Oog for a meal before the man departed. Sara was kind-hearted; she would probably agree to come to the leaving dinner. Sara liked delicious English food too.

'I've been meaning to ask if we could meet, Sara. I've been thinking of you lately.' Harry waited for a response, which didn't come, so he added, 'Beef Wellington is on the menu.'

'Beef Wellington?'

'Yes, Beef Wellington. Best I've ever eaten. And there are other wonderful things if you don't care for that.' But Harry knew BW was one of Sara's favourite dishes.

'I'd consider saying yes to the *bœuf*, but I want to say no to Oog.'

'Oh Sara please come. I understand that you're reluctant. I know Oog hits on you, but there is a good side to him, he's very clever and I want to stay in touch with him after he returns to Paris.'

'It's not so much that I don't like him, he's okay. I just find him a bit, well, oily, when he's had a few glasses of wine.'

'Yeah, he can be inappropriate. But if you don't join us, it'll be just myself, Bradley and Oog. I mean we'll get along, talk shop and all that stuff, but… Oh, I forgot to mention Bradley said he'd bring his new girlfriend on condition that you came too.'

'What? More blackmail? Food and a chance to meet Bradley's new girl?' Sara laughed.

'You can tell I'm desperate.'

'Let me think about it, Harry. I'll get back to you.'

Sara hung up. Harry sighed. The Red Lion had been his trump card. He wanted life to go back to how it had once been – just him, Sara, and that crazy cat of hers.

Would he have had an easier time persuading Sara to come to dinner if Oog hadn't been mentioned? A moot point, given there would be no dinner without Oog.

Be positive Harry told himself.

*****

Sara did agree to join them. Better still, she accepted his offer of a lift. Had to, really. Sara's only mode of transport was a bicycle. Fine around the city of Cambridge, but a drawback if you wanted to get to Soham, which was 20 miles away.

Bradley had agreed to pick up Oog from St Benedict's College, leaving Harry to collect Sara and have her all to himself until they got to the restaurant.

His phone rang just as he was leaving the flat. 'Bradley?'

'I'm only just leaving work, Harry. I won't have time to pick up Oog. Would you collect him, please? Sorry but I have to dash. Charlotte is waiting for me.'

Harry gritted his teeth. No chance of a nice private chat with Sara if Oog was in the car. 'Okay. If you arrive before us, the booking should be in my name.'

Storm Darragh was still blowing by the time they reached the Red Lion. The brunt had passed that morning, but the tricky storm threw out sudden gusts of wind, pushing cars sideways. Harry noticed Sara clutching the door handle a few times. Oog made syrupy comments from the back. Harry wished Oog at Jericho. If it had been just himself and Sara in the car, he could have reached out a hand to steady her, said soft things...

3

Johnny Rouse checked out the main restaurant room of the Red Lion as he drew a chair out for Rochelle. The Oak Room they'd called it when he'd phoned to book the table. It was bigger than he'd realised. He didn't recognise anyone. That was a relief. Rochelle would be looking down the room with just one table behind her. He'd quickly checked the four diners sitting there as he passed. Nah, he didn't know them. And Rochelle wasn't from Soham so she wouldn't know anyone. He hoped.

Sitting down, Johnny took another sly peek at the table occupants. Just to be sure. No, definitely strangers. Good. Three tables were empty. Maybe they'd stay that way.

He picked up the menu. Everything on it looked unfamiliar. A surge of panic made him think he needed the toilet. *Calm down...*

He'd never been to the Red Lion. Didn't usually go to restaurants, but he remembered being told that the food was special. He'd been curious to see how the old rundown pub had been renovated. Johnny looked around more slowly. He liked the interior. It had – what was that word? The one his snooty sister-in-law was always using? Oh yeah, *character.* There was a fire in the big old fireplace by the front door. Nice. And those old beams across the ceiling would appeal to Slaw. He dropped his head to hide a snigger. If his sister-in-law knew what he called her, she'd be furious. So would his wife. He never used that name around Tracy. If he'd realised how alike the sisters were before he'd married Tracy, he might have moved on, found someone else. He shuffled his menu, wriggled in his chair, coughed.

Rochelle stopped reading the menu. 'You okay there, Rousie?'

'Yeah.'

Johnny glanced at Rochelle. A real good looker and good in bed too. He was going to miss her but it had to end. Tonight. On a high. So the dinner had better be fancy.

Rochelle lifted her head again. 'Are you going to have a starter? We have to have a starter. Wait until I tell Sharon about this place. Really posh. She'll be so jealous. What are you going to have? What's *verde*?'

'What?'

'See there by the pulled pork? I've heard of pork, but...'

'I think it's like an opera or something. Slaw was yapping on about it the other week.'

Rochelle giggled. 'You'd better stop calling her that. Bet your wife hates you saying it.'

'I never say it in front of her.'

He was relieved, in some respects, to have come to the end of the affair. Rochelle was far too talkative.

A group of four came in. Johnny felt his heart rate speed up. That was... that was Tom Black. Shit. Johnny delivered and picked up from his yard. Shit!

Had Rochelle noticed? No her back was to that table.

Tom Black sat down on a chair by the wall. What if he turned and saw them? What if Tom knew Rochelle? Oh coming here was a mistake.

A troop of people came in, six at least. Johnny watched them stop by the dresser at the top of the room. They were laughing away. Oh no. Oh no! That was Natasha. Johnny lifted up his menu to hide his face.

How could this be happening to him? He didn't live in Soham. It should have been safe to come here but, not only was Tom Black here but now Natasha had come in as well. He hoped Rochelle wouldn't turn around. But she didn't know Natasha. Did she?

The group began to head off. She's turning back. She's nodding…

Oh no.

Feeling sick inside, Johnny held up his menu again. Was she looking at him? Shit shit. No wait… she's turning away. She's following the group into the other end of the restaurant. Was there another room down there? And was that… was that Fred? Ang… Anx? Fred Anxtey from… it must be. OMG he's nodding to Tom Black. Oh coming here was definitely a mistake. He should never have done posh, posh and popular… Oh…

'Are you ready to order?' A young woman stopped by their table.

Rochelle smiled up at her. 'Yes, and can we have wine? White please. I'm going to have the pulled pork with the verde and I'll have the turkey and for dessert, I'll have, let me see...'

The waitress spoke softly. 'I can take your dessert order later. Which wine have you chosen? Will it be a glass or a bottle?'

'Just a glass for me. Just white, any white. Make it a large one. He'll have a beer. He always drinks beer.'

Johnny raised his head, realised he was protected by the waitress's body. If he took his time. Ah it was okay. Natasha was gone now.

'Not a glass of wine, bring her a bottle.'

He hadn't decided what to eat. Too much was happening. The lines of print on the menu were wobbling. He squinted. 'Herring, and eh pork, no no eh, the turkey. I'll have the turkey too. Thanks. And a beer.'

The woman picked up the menus and began to walk past them towards the end of the room leading away from the front door. She stopped suddenly.

Had the waitress recognised him? Did she know he was married to Tracy? Did she know Tracy? Would she... he clutched his side as a gripping pain hit. No wait, wait... the girl was just turning around. She walked towards a corridor he'd noticed when they'd come in. Johnny hoped there wasn't another dining room in that direction. There were far too many people here already. Then he wondered if there were toilets down there. He was afraid to ask.

Coming here had been a massive mistake.

*****

Tom Black settled into the chair by the wall. It wasn't his usual table. He, Pammy and whoever was joining them generally sat at the big round table behind him. Table 14. It was empty. Had Donna been wrong to say it was booked? He would speak to her. Maybe it was free. He liked that table. Tom could sit with his back to the wall where he would be able to see everyone coming and going, and acknowledge those he knew.

He glanced at his wife. She'd been shifting in her seat since they'd sat down. The chair was smaller than the Winchester chairs at the big table. Another good reason to move tables. Pammy had put on a lot of weight lately. Bless her. He looked across at their guests. Ron Sparks and his wife. He'd forgotten Mrs Sparks's name already. Awkward, especially as she was sitting opposite him. Another large lady. She'd be better talking to his wife. If they couldn't move tables he'd swop places with Pammy.

Ah, there was Donna. He'd ask about moving once she was finished with the group of people who'd walked in.

Tom recognised some of them. He nodded at Fred Anstey. Weasel of a man that. Always whinging.

Natasha! What's she doing here? Surely she's not with Anstey? That won't last long. Natasha didn't have patience with whingers.

'Hello Tom, Pammy,' said Donna, coming over to them. 'Sorry we couldn't give you your usual table.'

'I see it's empty. Is it taken? Can we move?'

'Sorry Tom. It's booked.'

Donna turned as the front door opened. Another large group had arrived. 'Elsie will be along to take your order soon.'

Donna walked to her usual greeting point by a large dresser. Tom watched her speak to the crowd who had arrived.

Annoying about the table.

'Will you change places with me, Pammy? I'd prefer to be on the outside, to get to the toilet more easily. The old problem, you know.'

'What? Oh er yes.' Pammy heaved herself up to let him get by.

Tom saw her forehead wrinkle. Her eyebrows were creased together. He recognised that expression. She'd give him a telling off later. Pammy wasn't so much fun anymore.

As Tom stood up in the passageway between tables, he

noticed the couple by the window. Was that Johnny Rouse with his head in the menu? Who was he with? That wasn't his wife. Nice-looking young woman but definitely not Rousie's wife. Wasn't Mrs Rouse expecting? He'd ask Pammy about that later.

Tom sat down on the outside seat. This was much better. He'd felt squashed, sitting in by the wall.

Tom picked up the menu. The pulled pork and maybe the venison? It would be a change from the Beef Wellington.

'Well good evening Mr Black.'

Tom looked up. 'Good evening Ida, Wally,' said Tom, nodding to Ida and Wally Manners as they and four companions followed Donna to the end of the room. Difficult woman, Ida, but she was a district councillor so he had to stay in her good books.

Tom watched as they sat at an end table on the window side of the room.

Wasn't that young Leonard and his fancy wife? Tom really did wish he was sitting at the usual table. He liked people-watching. There was a good mix here this evening.

For some reason, Ida was tittering all over Paul Leonard's wife. Ida Manners never did anything without a motive. She was always looking for some kind of benefit. She wouldn't get that from Paul Leonard, so it must be his wife she was focussing on. Had Tom heard a rumour that the woman was planning to open a new hair salon? Kylie – that was her name. Nice looking. Too elegant for Paul?

Another couple arrived. Donna led them to the table beside Tom. He sighed. No chance of a move now. The Oak Room was almost full.

The door opened again. More people. Who's bringing that smile to Donna's face? Ah, Harry Meredith. Handsome chap. Hadn't Harry been in the news recently?

A stabbing? A gun fight? The chap looked fine, so perhaps Tom was mis-remembering. He nodded as Harry and his companions passed by and sat just behind Tom.

This might be a good chance to pick up some police gossip. Tom leaned back in his chair, heard Harry introduce the young woman with– Hold on, he knew that chap too. Yes, Bradley West. Met him at some function. Countryside Watch was it?

Harry and Bradley were from Cambridge. Weren't they a bit off their patch here in Soham? Hmm, the Red Lion's reputation must be spreading.

4

Sara was relieved when they left the blowy A14 behind. Storm Darragh still had some power left. She and Harry hadn't talked much on the drive. That gave her time to observe him.

She noticed new lines on his face. He seemed sad. She wondered what had caused the change from his usual happy self. He wasn't as bright and lively as he'd once been. And he was favouring his left arm, letting it rest on his thigh at times. Sara knew he'd been wounded trying to disarm a man with a knife. There was no chance to check things out, however, with Oog commenting on everything from the back seat. He even explained the weather to them. She supposed he'd temporarily forgotten that her area of research at the University was climate change. She reminded herself that the evening was all about Oog so she smiled at the odd comment and pretended not to hear some of the irritating ones.

Finally, they arrived. It was lovely to get in out of the wind. 'What a gorgeous fire,' she said, spotting it near the entrance. She stopped by a small Christmas tree just inside the door. It was hung with dried orange segments. Sara sniffed. 'Oh the smells! Food and Christmas spices. Gorgeous,' she said to Harry. 'And when do you see a real wood fire these days?' She looked around. 'This room is wonderful. I love the oak beams.'

A woman came to greet them. She gave Harry a hug. 'Hello my lovely. How's your arm?'

'Good.'

'Splendid. You'll be able to feed yourself.'

Harry laughed.

'Your friends are here already.' Donna pointed to her right.

Sara saw Bradley sitting with, she presumed, Charlotte. Sara waved.

'Donna, this is Sara.'

Sara hadn't expected to be introduced. The woman's friendly smile became a wide grin. Harry must be well known here. Hmm. Things she didn't know about Harry.

Sara looked down the long room. Bradley and Charlotte were sitting at a round table opposite the window wall. As they approached, Bradley pulled out a chair, placing her next to him. Harry sat on her other side. Sara's back was partly to the wall and partly against a section of open wood panelling which divided the long room. It gave her a view of everything. She leaned across Bradley to greet Charlotte, who seemed shy.

Now that she was able to relax, Sara admitted that it was lovely to see Harry. She had missed him. Over a year apart now. They had never discussed the way their relationship had ended because Harry went to London after the kidnapped girl was found. But Sara guessed after she saw Harry and Maria together. It had been impossible to mistake the vibe between them. When the distressing circumstances of how that poor girl had been kept captive came out, Sara knew that Harry would have suffered. But still, running off with someone else was not what she had expected him to do.

The affair had soon blown over, but the damage lingered.

Seeing Harry now and recognising that old tug towards him, she realised that time had softened her negative feelings. But she remembered the hurt, so remnants of them hung around, like cobwebs you didn't see before walking into them. She ran her fingers through her hair, as though to check and clear any clinging cobwebs.

Sara let her eyes linger on Harry. Still handsome, even if he was looking older. He was chatting to Oog as they read the menu. He was more relaxed than he'd been in the car. Reluctant as she was to admit it, she loved looking at Harry. Still loved him, in fact. Sara turned away.

To distract herself, she looked around the restaurant. It was quite unique. A long room, soft white paint on the walls which set off the old time-worn beams. Sara stretched out her hand to touch the timber of the open wood section. She wondered if it had once been filled in. Had the building been a house before?

Restaurant sounds of cutlery clinking, glasses ringing, soft talk and louder voices, laughter, made her look around the room.

Every table was full, everyone seemed happy. Ah, wait, not everyone. A man at a table for six, at the far end of the dining room, was staring down towards the fire by the entrance. He wasn't engaging with his table companions. They were busy talking together. He dropped his head to his phone, and then looked up again. Sara tried to follow his line of vision. She couldn't see what had drawn his attention, but she noticed a step up to another dining room.

A line of bobbing heads was visible through the gap in the doorway. There must be a group in there. Faint sounds of laughter drifted out. Was he looking at someone in there?

Donna came to take their order.

'Have you decided what to have, my lovelies?'

There was much merry laughter as they made their choices and ordered drinks. Harry gave Sara a huge beaming smile when Donna left. She couldn't help herself grinning back. The atmosphere was lovely, Harry seemed happy.

'Ah, Sara,' Oog leaned across Harry to pass her the basket of bread. 'I am very pleased you agreed to join us. Harry per'aps you would move so I can sit close to *la belle* Sara?'

Harry stayed just where he was.

Sara dropped her head to hide a smile and turned to Bradley. Charlotte was leaning in towards him. They seemed oblivious of herself, Harry and Oog. Sara felt a twinge of sadness, remembering the exciting feeling she'd had when she and Harry had first met.

Their starters arrived.

Because she was having Beef Wellington, Sara had chosen a light starter – goat's cheese salad. Harry and Bradley chose pulled pork, Charlotte smoked salmon pâté. Oog had ordered crevettes.

Sara watched him lick his lips as the plate of giant prawns was placed in front of him. The starter should keep him busy for a while and she might have a chance to chat with Harry.

'How's your salad?' Harry asked.

'Lovely. Are you enjoying the pork?'

'Very much.'

She didn't know what to say to him. It used to be so easy between them.

'How is Arabella?'

Dear dear, thought Sara, things were bad if Harry had to ask about her cat.

'He's fine.'

Oog leaned across. 'Arabella? 'ee? But Harry, do you make a mistake? That is a girl's name *n'est pas*?'

'You're correct, Oog. Arabella is a girl's name and Sara did say 'he' because her cat is a boy cat.'

'*Mon dieu!*'

Oog wiped a spot of mayonnaise from one corner of his mouth, and missed the second on the other side. Sara swallowed a grin. He'd demolished all the crevettes.

A man at the next table stood, shoving his chair noisily back. Hadn't he nodded at Harry as they came in? She supposed Harry knew all sorts of people.

A woman came out of the far room.

As Sara watched, the man quickly walked around his table. He and the woman almost collided. Strangely, the man didn't give way. Oops, manners! They both turned down the corridor – to visit the bathroom, Sara assumed.

The woman had reminded Sara of her mother. Same build, same hair. Mum's had grown coarser and wirier as she entered her fifties. She hated how her hair had changed. Sara didn't; she thought Mum looked lovely.

In her peripheral vision, Sara saw the angry man from the far end of the room, almost run after the woman and the man. It was unusual to see people running in a restaurant.

'What's at the end of that corridor?' she asked Harry. 'Another dining room?'

'Um,' Harry leaned back to let the waitress remove his plate. 'No, the bar is down there, toilets and a bar.'

Bradley leaned towards Charlotte. 'Would you like to come here, after Christmas? We could start off in the bar.'

'Oh yes,' she said. The pair drifted back to leaning close and whispering.

As Sara turned away from the lovebirds, a young man from the nearby table suddenly got up and also went down the corridor. The toilets and bar were popular! The man was clutching a phone. The young woman he'd been sitting with turned her head to watch him walk away. She shrugged and went back to sipping her glass of wine.

Sara was about to speak to Harry when a young woman from the end table, the one who'd been sitting opposite that angry young man passed by. She marched down the corridor too. The woman had perfectly cut sleek black hair and a fringe. She reminded Sara of Cleopatra.

Heavens, a lot of people were moving about.

As Bradley and Charlotte had withdrawn from the group again, Sara felt she really ought to help Harry out with Oog.

'Are you happy to be going back to France soon? Do you have plans for Christmas?'

'Yes, I go home to my town near Toulouse. We have wonderful times there. Toulouse, it comes alive at Christmas. Markets, they are–' Oog pinched his thumb and middle finger together, 'they are superb. Not like the Cambridge markets which are just so so. We have *Les Ramblas*–'

'*Las Ramblas*? I thought that was in Barcelona?'

'*Mais non, ma chère* Sara, it is different. In Toulouse it is "Les". *Plus d'ambiance que Barcelone.*'

Oh, thought Sara, *have I insulted him?* But Oog chatted on, mostly to Harry.

Before long their main courses were brought out.

More delicious smells. Sara savoured them. Harry and Bradley had also chosen Beef Wellington. Oog didn't. Perhaps he was being patriotic. After all, Wellington had trounced the French at Waterloo. Whatever the reason, Oog had chosen venison.

Sara tucked into her meal. It was wonderful, as were the roast potatoes – crispy and soft as butter beneath the crunch. If only she'd cycled – it would take her ages to work off all the delicious calories.

'Are you enjoying the *bœuf*?' asked Harry.

'I certainly am. Are you?'

'Ditto.'

'And you, Oog?' she asked. 'Are you enjoying your venison'

'*C'est délicieux*.'

Halfway through her meal, Sara looked up. Donna was standing by that lovely old dresser. Her happy face had changed. She looked pale and she shook. She seemed to be staring at Harry.

'Something's wrong,' whispered Sara, laying down her knife and tugging at Harry's sleeve. 'Look at Donna's face.'

*****

Harry glanced up. Donna stood where she often did to greet arrivals, by the dresser at the start of the corridor which led to the bar. Her eyes were dark orbs in a colourless face. She was staring at him. Harry thought she was trying to speak, to send him a message. Her lips moved but there was no sound.

He rose, slipped around the back of Oog's chair, and crossed to stand in front of Donna so the other diners wouldn't see her distress.

'What is it?'

Up close, she looked even more upset. She raised her right hand. It shook. Her index finger seemed to be pointing down the corridor. Harry leaned to one side. He saw the edge of someone sitting on the big sofa. They appeared to be asleep.

But a sleeping customer wouldn't create such a reaction in the ever-calm, ever-cool Donna.

Harry strode down the corridor.

5

Harry stepped into the bar. Noise from the restaurant rooms was muted here. The lighting was low. The woman on the sofa was the only person present. She was leaning towards the wall on her left. There was a stillness to her, no rising or falling of her chest as she breathed.

'Hello,' he called.

She didn't answer. Didn't move. Was she asleep?

Harry turned to draw across the heavy velvet curtain which separated the bar from the corridor. Donna was standing at the end, watching him. He raised his index finger to signal one minute. She nodded her understanding and stayed where she was. Thank goodness he had come to know Donna, and the Red Lion so well, that he knew he could trust her and rely on her.

In all his years of being a detective, Harry had never been in a situation where a death had occurred while he was out socialising. He felt a tightness in his chest akin to a panic attack. He felt like a new recruit.

But he wasn't.

Harry stood before the woman who looked to be in her fifties. Something about her seemed familiar. What was it? Ah, her hair. She reminded him of Sara's mother. They had the same kind of wiry fluffy hair. This woman's hair was dark brown and showing strands of grey. It was tied at the back of her neck.

He leaned down and moved a hand in front of her nose and mouth. As he expected, there was no warmth of exhaled air. Harry checked his inside jacket pocket and pulled out the pair of disposable gloves he always carried. Drawing them on, he placed two fingers on the woman's neck, by the carotid artery. There was no pulse.

Using his covered leg, Harry pushed the coffee table in front of the sofa slightly aside, giving him room to stand by the body. He slowly checked for wounds. The woman might have died of natural causes. It might simply be a case of calling a doctor for verification, and contacting the local police to handle the death.

Where was the nearest local police station? Ely, probably. Six, maybe seven miles away?

Harry leaned towards the woman's body and lifted one of her eyelids. Her eyes were brown. Given the colour, it wasn't easy to see the pupil but Harry thought it was dilated. He took out his phone, pressed the torch function and shone the light into her eye. The size of the pupil didn't change, as it would have if she'd been alive. He moved his slow scrutiny to her neck, chest, midriff, wait–were those spots of blood on her left side? Gently probing the area revealed a tear in the woman's dress.

Harry whistled silently. That looked like a stab wound. A small amount of blood had soaked into the edges of the tear. This woman had been killed.

He sat a moment, breathing in. He could smell lemons and a spirit – brandy?

The woman had been alive and probably enjoying herself just a short while ago. Had she come to the bar for a drink? Had she been meeting someone? Donna might know. He should bring her down to the bar. Was anyone missing from the tables? Donna would help with that too.

As he rose from the coffee table Harry's foot caught on something. Looking down, he saw a handbag. He opened it, found the purse, laid it on the coffee table and teased out a driving licence.

He examined the photo and name: Natasha Poole. An Ely address. Natasha. The photo was like enough to the woman to prove who she was, though someone would have to identify her formally.

Harry replaced the licence and returned the purse to the handbag. He moved to the curtain but slowed as he went to draw it.

What was he to do? Technically, he was out socially so he shouldn't investigate. Additionally, he was a potential witness and should stand back for that reason also. But he was here, on the spot. He didn't know what resources or personnel Ely had and ultimately the investigation would go to Cambridge and to Harry's team.

If in doubt…

Harry tapped DCI Fountain's number on his phone.

She answered immediately. 'Harry? It's Saturday evening. Has something happened?'

'It has, Ma'am. I'm in a restaurant in Soham. The Red Lion.'

'Why are you phoning me?'

'One of the diners has been murdered. A woman. I'm here with Bradley and Hugues Dubois. I know all the reasons for standing back but I'm on the spot, Ma'am. It's likely one of the diners killed this woman.'

'Hmmm,' said the DCI.

Harry waited.

'You say DS West is with you, and our visiting scholar, Hugues Dubois, who is an officer with the *Sûreté* in Paris.' She pronounced Oog's name as the French do. 'Okay, that counts as a team. Make a start on the investigation but be ready to pass it to whoever is free in Cambridge if you want to stand down. I'll alert them to send an Incident Van, ambulance and back-up. And we'll ask Ely to get a squad car over there asap. There's no longer a police presence in Soham.' The DCI took a deep breath. 'Harry,' she stopped talking. 'You are to step back immediately if you find…'

Harry broke into the conversation. 'I will Ma'am. I can assure you of that. I can also assure you that I feel perfectly capable. My injury is mostly healed and it will not be a problem. And Bradley is here.'

'Hmm. Keep me updated. Is that clear?'

The investigation was going to be a challenge. For Harry and Bradley, because it was out of their normal field of work, and Harry was conscious of the extra layer of scrutiny from DCI Fountain. For Lucy, Donna and their staff who would be distressed to say the least. And how would the customers feel? They, like himself, had come to the Red Lion to relax and enjoy themselves. It was less than three weeks to Christmas. What could he do to lessen the distress? He thought of Sara and Charlotte. Especially of Sara.

Once the crime was called in, a team would come out. He thought it would take the team about half an hour or so to get to Soham. Help from Ely should arrive far faster.

Good. He would set them to manage the customers as soon as they got here.

What could be done in the meantime? Because Natasha Poole's body was still warm, it was likely the killer was still in the restaurant.

Harry felt an uptick in his heartbeat. Adrenalin kicking in. He breathed in and out slowly to lessen the affect.

He must ask Donna if anyone had left. Would she know? Probably. Harry had often been struck by the sense of community in the Red Lion, the easy camaraderie between the staff, especially Donna, and the customers. Would Bradley and Oog be able to contain the inquiry? At least he had a team. That in itself was a minor miracle.

Harry's first job was to secure the building. He needed Donna for that. For a lot of things, actually.

Harry was forming a plan of action as he stepped back through the curtain. He beckoned to Donna who came swiftly down the corridor.

'Is she dead Harry?'

'Yes. Did you recognise her, Donna?'

'No. What did she die of?'

Harry spoke as gently as he could. 'It wasn't an accident.'

She stared at him, her eyes growing wider and wider, her jaw dropping. Donna placed a hand in front of her mouth. 'No!'

'I believe the woman has been killed.'

'Killed? As in… killed?' Donna backed against the corridor wall.

Harry put a hand out to steady her. 'Yes.' He gave her a moment to take in the enormity of what had happened. 'I will need your help to contain this because the killer will most likely be one of the diners.'

Donna took in deep breath, and let it out slowly. 'What? No! Oh Harry, I hope you're mistaken.'

'I want to speak to Lucy and to you, but the first and most important thing to do is to secure the entrance. Will you do that, please? I'm going to bring my colleague, Bradley West, down and we will work out how to proceed.'

'What about people who want to leave?'

"They can't leave at present. Sorry,' he said, watching Donna's reaction. 'I know that will be difficult. We will address that, but first things first. Secure the doors, then ask Lucy to come into the corridor. You can tell her what has happened when you get her on her own, but don't tell anyone else. Is there CCTV, by the way?'

'No.'

'Pity. It would have made the investigation easier. I'm going to get Bradley, DS West.'

Donna walked back to the Oak Room. She moved out of Harry's line of view, but returned swiftly. He watched her walk to the front door. She locked it.

Harry followed, stopped at the end of the corridor and looked right to his table.

Sara noticed him. He gave her an almost imperceptible nod. She frowned. He angled his head towards Bradley. Like Donna, Sara's eyes opened wide. She tapped Bradley's arm. When he looked up, she inclined her head towards Harry.

Stepping back into the corridor, Harry thanked his lucky stars for the sensitive Sara. She had always picked up on tiny cues.

Bradley stood up, squeezed Charlotte's arm and excused himself. He followed Harry to the bar. They slipped behind the curtain.

6

Bradley stood inside the bar curtain. He looked dumbfounded. 'The woman isn't dead, Harry? Is she?'

'She is.'

Bradley moved closer to Natasha Poole's body. 'Things like this just don't happen. We're on a night out!'

'Not anymore.' Harry shook his head. 'I didn't notice anything going on. Not until Sara drew my attention to Donna, who was standing by the dresser and looking… devastated.'

'Neither did I, mate. I was focussed mainly on Charlotte and paying a bit of attention to you, Sara and Oog.'

'Yes. That's what we were here to do. I was so far from work mode that my antennae were completely shut down. This is a shock.'

'Is there CCTV?'

'No. I asked Donna.'

'Someone must have seen something, Harry. Someone must have noticed who went down the corridor.'

'Yes, but where might they have been going? To the

toilets? To take trays back to the kitchen? To murder? We have a mountain to climb, Bradley.'

Bradley patted Harry on the shoulder. 'It's a rotten turn to the evening, but we have a dead woman and it's up to us to find out who killed her. I actually feel guilty that we were intent on socialising while this was happening, but we can work to find out who killed her.'

'We can and we will do our best,' said Harry. 'I've spoken to DCI Fountain. She's given us the go ahead to work on the case. A team and Incident Van will head out from Cambridge shortly. She said she would arrange for Ely Station to send a squad car.'

'Right.' Bradley, who had also donned disposable gloves, examined the body. 'Looks like she's been stabbed. Here?' He pointed to the spotting of blood just above the woman's waist.

'Yes. I came to the same conclusion.'

Bradley stood up. Looked slowly around the bar.

'This is going to be tricky,' said Harry. 'The killer is likely still to be in the restaurant. I've asked Donna to secure the entrance. We will need someone to guard it and also someone to guard the entrance to the corridor and bar, while we wait for the PCs to arrive from Ely.'

'Wow, this is a first. Do you have ideas on how to manage this?'

'Some. The biggest challenge will be keeping what's happened quiet as long as we can. We have to do that to prevent panic. There are a lot of people here this evening. Ultimately, we will need to interview, or at least speak, to all of them.'

'Do the restaurant owners, the chef, the staff know what's happened?'

'Donna, the front of house manager, is the one who found the body.'

'Do you suspect her?'

'No.'

'We need to keep an open mind, Harry.'

'I'm aware of that, and we will question them, however I've known Donna and Lucy the chef/ proprietor for a long time. I haven't spoken to Lucy yet but I can't imagine them committing murder in their own restaurant.'

A whispered 'Harry?' filtered through the curtain.

Harry stepped into the corridor.

Donna and Lucy were waiting for him. Donna had recovered some of her colour. It was Lucy who now looked pale and shocked.

'Are you sure the woman is dead?'

'I am. Would you glance at her, please, Lucy? You might know her.'

'Oh Harry, I don't think I can do that.'

'Please, Lucy. We need to know if you recognise her.'

Harry twitched the curtain back. Lucy crept into the bar. She looked a moment at Natasha Poole, shivered, and quickly backed into the corridor.

'No. I don't know her. Poor woman. What an awful thing to happen. But why was she killed here? I can't believe it. I can't understand why it would happen, especially in a restaurant.'

Harry closed the curtain across the entrance again.

Lucy stood by Donna. 'When, when will you, you move the body?'

'I've spoken to my Chief Inspector. A scene-of-crime team is on the way. They should be here in half an hour or so.'

'Half an hour? That's a very long time. What about all the people, the customers?'

Just then, one of the serving staff came down the corridor carrying plates. She came to a halt at the door to the kitchen. 'So what's going on?' she asked. 'That curtain is never drawn.'

'Go through to the kitchen, Agnes,' said Donna, moving towards the young woman and waiting until the door had closed behind her.

'Lucy,' said Harry, 'this area needs to be cordoned off. Will you organise for the serving staff to use the door leading out of the kitchen into the end of the Oak Room, please? '

'But… Okay. And then? I'm going to have to tell the staff something.'

'Yes,' said Donna, 'and the customers.'

'We can't tell them the truth because it may spread panic. We need a story for now. Tell the staff there's been an accident and that this corridor is out of bounds for the present. It is now a crime scene. Our next priority is to search for the murder weapon.'

Lucy and Donna clutched each other. They were trembling.

Could he do anything to help them? Soften the blow? No. Crime was cruel, especially murder. The investigation took priority.

Bradley stepped out from the bar and stood by Harry.

'This is Detective Sergeant Bradley West. He is, was, part of my dining group this evening.'

Lucy stared. 'Oh. Two policemen?'

'Talk about right place right time,' said Donna.

'You mentioned searching for the murder weapon, Harry,' said Bradley.

'Yes. We're looking for a knife. Donna, will you come into the bar with me, please? I need you to check if anything is missing there. Lucy, will you go back to the kitchen and suspend access into this corridor?'

Lucy left them, looking back over her shoulder as she

returned to the kitchen.

Donna followed Harry and Bradley into the bar. She looked briefly at Natasha Poole's body, then busied herself looking around. It took her moments to notice that the knife for cutting up lemons was missing.

'It's always there,' she pointed to a plate of cut lemons.

'Have a good search behind the bar but don't touch anything. Point it out to us. Make sure the knife isn't in a different place, or that it hasn't fallen on the floor or behind a cupboard.'

While Donna slowly examined the bar area, Harry and Bradley checked the rest of the space. They found nothing on the table, seats, nor on the floor – apart from Natasha Poole's handbag.

'It's not here, Harry. It's definitely gone. Do you think it was the…'

'It's likely. Describe it to us, please?'

'It's small and very sharp.'

'How small?'

'Six, maybe seven inches long? It's serrated on one side and has a black plastic handle.'

'Bradley, will you search the toilets, please, starting with the one nearest the main restaurant room, and work back towards the bar?'

'I'd better get my Scene-of-Crime box from the car,' said Bradley. 'We're going to need it. Can we open this fire exit, Donna? Is there a route to the car park? Will an alarm go off if I open it?'

'I'll disable the alarm for the present. You can't get to the car park that way, but you can go out through the kitchen. A door leads from there to the road and the car park.'

'And is that door kept locked?' asked Harry.

'No.'

'Would you lock it as soon as Bradley returns, please?'

'What about fire regulations? And what about the staff? They'll want to know who Bradley is, and why he's cutting through the kitchen. '

'Tell them Bradley is helping with the accident and we'll come and talk to you all soon. I understand what you say about fire regulations, that door must stay unlocked. But tell the staff they mustn't use it except in an emergency.'

Looking unhappy, Donna went off with Bradley.

When they returned, Bradley placed the SoC box on the table.

'We're short on people until help arrives,' said Harry. 'We need someone to stand guard on the front door while we wait for help to arrive from Ely.'

Should he ask Oog to take on that job? No, he'd prefer to ask Oog to take on a policing role.

'I don't want any of our staff to do that,' said Donna. 'What if there was trouble?'

'We have to put someone by the door, though.'

'Em, there's a man we know dining here this evening, Geoff. He might help us.'

'Who's Geoff?'

'He's with the big party in the Victorian Room – the dining room on the far side of the fireplace? Geoff's been coming here for years. I trust him.'

'Do you mean Geoff Norman, by any chance?' asked Bradley.

'Yes. Do you know him?'

Bradley turned to Harry. 'I met him through Countryside Watch. He's a local farmer. He's very active in the community. I think we can trust him to help.'

'I suppose. And the door is locked. Okay. Donna, will you bring him down to see me? Discreetly, of course.'

'Okay.'

'Oh and Donna?' Harry called her back. 'When you've done that, will you check if anyone's missing from the restaurant rooms?'

Donna wriggled her shoulders. 'But how will I… It's okay, I'll check for gaps. If a table isn't full...'

'Sounds good, Donna.'

Off she went.

Harry waited by the curtain. Donna soon came back, accompanied by a man who was joking and laughing with her.

'So what's this 'job' you want me to do, Donna? Does it mean I'll get double dessert?'

'Geoff Norman, this is Harry Meredith. He will explain.'

7

Sara was trying to adjust to the way the evening had changed. Harry and Bradley had gone off. They would not have done so unless something had happened. Something serious. A crime. In a restaurant? During dinner? Unbelievable.

She glanced at Charlotte, who seemed confused and upset. Sara tapped the seat that Bradley had vacated. 'Sit here, Charlotte. It will be easier to talk if we're closer.'

Charlotte looked back towards the corridor. 'But... if Bradley comes back?'

'Then you can move seats again, of course.' Sara smiled, hoping to ease Charlotte's evident distress at being abandoned without a word.

Oh police work! It had taken Harry from her side many times. Sara had learned to live with it, to continue with her own life and not to brood about being left. When Harry was called away, he simply had to go.

If only his disappearing off with Maria could have been explained in the same way.

Sara patted the seat again. Charlotte moved onto it.

Next to Sara, Oog slid into Harry's vacant seat. 'We have been abandoned,' he said.

'Not abandoned,' replied Sara, 'simply missing two of our party. They will probably return quite soon.' Sara didn't really believe that, but she wanted to spare Charlotte undue worry.

'Harry and Bradley must have work to do. They would not leave us otherwise, I am sure. I envy them,' said Oog. 'I miss my own work. It has been good to be in Cambridge, and there has been much to learn at the Institute, but me, I prefer action to words.'

Why did Sara find it difficult to think of Oog as a man of action? Perhaps because, every time she saw him, he was sitting and talking. 'You do?'

'Yes. Here I must take the place of a student and that is not easy for me when I know so much.'

Ah. Oog was still Oog, a little vain and a little full of himself. Sara turned to Charlotte.

'We've never had a proper chance to talk, Charlotte, so I don't know where you work, or what you like to do.'

'Oh I'm just from Cambridge. I don't have an important job like Bradley or Harry. I work in an advertising agency, producing artwork for ads. So boring really.'

'*Mais non*,' said Oog, leaning closer. 'This is so interesting. And did you study art?'

Sara leaned back in her chair, both to avoid getting too close to Oog, but also because there was still a spot of mayonnaise on his chin and it made her feel a little queasy. Thank goodness it was dill mayonnaise and not garlic. Would he be offended if she pointed it out? Sara abandoned the idea because he was engaging with Charlotte and taking her mind off Bradley.

'I studied at the Cambridge School of Art, but I left

after two years. Most of the people in my year were so much better than I was.'

'*Mais non*, Charlotte, I cannot believe that to be true. You have such style. This dress you are wearing, it is so chic, and this, this, this – is it a cardigan? The colour is *magnifique* with the dress.'

Charlotte blushed. Sara thought he was overdoing it.

'Do you have an interest in the arts, Oog?' Sara asked.

'I go to many galleries and exhibitions in Paris. And I tell you, *chère* Charlotte, that we must all begin somewhere and I think that you will be learning a lot at your work though you might not feel *sympatique* with the advertising.'

'Umm, no, I don't. Working in advertising is not what I wanted to do, but it's a job and I have to work. What about you, Sara?'

'I'm a lecturer at the University of Cambridge.'

'What do you lecture in?'

'Environmental Science.'

'Oh, right.'

Charlotte's eyes seemed to glaze over. Sara was used to this reaction. She understood. It could be a controversial subject. Some people crumpled their foreheads while listening and she occasionally imagined they saw her as an activist. Several had looked her up and down, as though searching for evidence of the orange paint or powder that activists often used during protests. But she wasn't an activist. She was a serious academic. Maybe not always serious.

Oog came to her rescue. 'Yes, Sara, I have been to one of your lectures.'

Sara was mildly shocked. She hadn't seen him in the main lecture hall. Perhaps he'd hidden at the back.

'*Mai oui*,' he said, acknowledging her stare. 'I do not know much about climate change but the students, they were so noisy and asking so many questions. They were, how do you say? challenging? but you answered every question. You are an expert.'

Oog looked beyond Sara at Charlotte, who had begun moving food around on her plate. 'You too, Charlotte, will be expert soon. You must keep working and drawing.'

Donna had returned. As Sara watched, she took a key from a drawer of the big dresser, went to the front door and locked it.

She locked it. They were all locked in!

Goodness what on earth had happened?

Donna went back down the corridor. Sara shivered. Whatever had happened, it was going to affect everyone in the restaurant.

'Sara, you are cold?' Oog rubbed her arm. 'Do you have a scarf? I will get it for you.'

'Oh, no, it was just a momentary thing. Thank you, Oog, no need for a scarf.'

Sara looked at the remains of her Beef Wellington. She had lost her appetite. She wished Harry would come back and tell her what was going on.

Donna soon returned but she went into the other dining room on the far side of the fireplace. Oog and Charlotte were deep in a conversation about art, painting, drawing and she hardly knew what.

Oog was glancing at her every now and then. Of course he knew something was going on. How could he not? He was covering his curiosity well.

Donna emerged from the far dining room with a man who seemed in good form. He was chatting and laughing. Donna was trying to smile but failing to make the smile last. They vanished into the corridor.

Charlotte was finishing her meal. Sara glanced at Oog. He raised his eyebrows. Donna's trek to the front door hadn't passed him by either.

The diners seemed oblivious to the mystery proceedings. Almost everyone was busy chatting, laughing, eating. Almost.

A woman at the end table was fiddling with her knife and turning her head to look around. Her hair gleamed under the lights. Hadn't she and the young man opposite her, gone down the corridor earlier? It was her. Sara remembered her looking like Cleopatra.

The man across from her was staring out the window, completely disengaged from his table companions.

The couple at the table for two across the aisle, were arguing in low voices. Hadn't that young man left his table also? Oh dear. What a shame. Christmas was so near.

Sara's immediate neighbour, the older man with oiled hair, who'd shoved his chair back so noisily earlier, seemed more settled now. Sara caught him looking at her. She kept her nerve and he looked away.

Wait, thought Sara, the woman whom he'd collided with – she hadn't returned to the other dining room. Sara was sure of that because the woman had reminded Sara of her mother. Sara's mother lived in Devon and Sara didn't see half as much of her as she would have liked. She'd felt a sharp sense of longing when she spotted the Mum-lookalike earlier. She was sure she would have noticed that woman returning.

Was whatever had happened connected to her?

The jolly man who'd gone down the corridor with Donna returned. He was no longer smiling. He seemed distressed. As Sara watched, he hesitated at the entrance to the other dining room, as though he wanted to go back there. Instead, he walked to the front door, turned his back to it and stood there. Was he on guard? He fished out his mobile phone. Sara thought his hands shook.

'You are not finishing your *boeuf*, Sara. It was not good?'

Startled, Sara automatically lifted her knife and fork. 'It's very good. I, I… Was the turkey good, Charlotte?'

'It was lovely.' Charlotte finished up the last of her meal.

Sara laid her knife and fork back down. Her appetite was completely gone. She felt sick. She reached for the jug of water.

Harry appeared at the end of the corridor. Sara's heart lifted. He came over to their table. Oog began to stand up, ready to give his seat back to Harry.

'It's okay, Oog.' Harry sat into Oog's vacant chair. 'I won't be staying.'

8

Harry glanced at Charlotte. He didn't know Bradley's new girl very well and didn't want to startle her. It would definitely be best to stick with the accident story for now.

Feeling Sara's keen gaze, Harry looked at the three of them. 'There's been an accident.'

Charlotte gulped.

Although Harry had barely spoken above a whisper, a man sitting at the table beside them, Tom Black, turned to stare. Impressive, thought Harry. The man must be able to hear the grass grow.

Tom Black's table was at the end of the corridor and Tom was facing towards it. Harry had met him at a policing event. The man must have noticed some, at least, of the comings and goings. He could be a useful witness. Harry tucked the thought away.

'How awful,' said Sara, 'so close to Christmas when people are out to enjoy themselves. What can you tell us?'

'Not very much at the moment.'

'Where's Bradley?' asked Charlotte.

'He's helping down the other end.'

'At the bar?'

'Yes.'

Harry needed to get away before Charlotte asked awkward questions. 'Oog, you know a bit about…,' Harry coughed, 'about cardio… will you come with me and give us a hand?'

Oog leapt up. Harry was only surprised that Oog hadn't pushed to be involved sooner.

* * * * *

Oog stood inside the bar curtain, looking at the dead woman.

'What happened?'

Harry outlined what they had discovered so far. 'A team is coming from Cambridge but,' he checked his watch, 'it will be twenty minutes, maybe half an hour or so before they arrive. I want to start questioning the diners, ready to let them go as soon as we clear them. Bradley is searching the toilets for the murder weapon.'

Harry knew about Oog's background. Harry's boss, DCI Fountain, was Oog's sponsor for his fellowship in Cambridge. Oog was an officer with the *Sûreté* in Paris. While Harry couldn't involve him directly in the investigation, because he had no official standing in the UK, Oog could help and clearly he was keen to.

'Bradley and I will start talking to the diners very soon, and draw aside people we would like to question more thoroughly. We'll do that once Bradley finishes his search.'

Oog examined the bar, paying close attention to Natasha Poole's body. 'What is the murder weapon?'

'We believe it's a small sharp knife with a serrated edge and a black handle. It was used for cutting up lemons to put in drinks.'

'Ah, lemons. I could search for this knife then Bradley would be free to work with you, *non*?'

Great. Harry had hoped Oog would volunteer. 'Thank you, Oog. There are disposable gloves in this box and evidence bags. You will also need to photograph everything before you search and when and if you find anything of interest.' Harry smiled to soften the request. He was sure Oog knew very well what to do.

'Yes yes, I understand. Which camera do we use?'

There wasn't a camera in the SoC box. Harry didn't want to hand over his phone, nor Bradley's, as both would be needed. Oog's phone would doubtless be French, which would create jurisdictional issues and… wait, he could ask Sara if they might borrow hers.

'I'm going to get Sara's phone. We could use that.'

'*Oui d'accord*.'

Harry sped down to the Oak Room and over to his table. He saw the surprise on Sara's face as he sat down beside her. He lowered his voice. 'Sweetheart, may I borrow your phone? Oog needs to take photos.'

'You want to give Oog my phone?'

'Please Sara.'

Charlotte was staring at him. Damn.

He leaned closer to Sara's ear and whispered. 'There's been a murder. Oog is going to search for the weapon and take photos. But his phone is French and the investigation is in the UK.'

'Ah. Okay I understand.' Sara fished her phone out, unlocked it, opened the photo app, and handed it over saying, 'I hope he likes cat photos. The unlock code is Mum's birth year. Do you remember what that is?'

'I do. Her 50th birthday party during the Covid pandemic was unforgettable. Thirty of us, in chilly Devon. It was lucky it fell towards the end of 2021.'

Harry could have kissed Sara, so relieved was he to get the camera. Instead, he sped back to the bar.

'Here is Sara's phone. The unlock code is 1971.' Harry felt some trepidation handing the open phone to Oog, but he had to trust the man.

'*Merci*, I will keep the lovely Sara's privacy in mind as I take the photos.'

'Great. Have a good look around here, Oog before you leave in case you spot something we've missed. While you're doing that, I'll fetch Bradley.'

Oog corroborated what Harry and Bradley had and hadn't found, in the bar. Soon Oog, wearing gloves and carrying Sara's phone, set off for the toilets.

* * * * *

Harry knocked at the kitchen door and entered. The washing up area was empty. He found Lucy, Donna, Agnes and two other members of staff in the kitchen. 'Lucy, Donna, may I have a word?'

They followed him out to the corridor.

'Right,' he said, 'we're making some progress.'

'Have you found the killer?' asked Donna.

'No, but we're moving along with the investigation. Our French colleague, Hugues Dubois, call him Oog, is searching for the knife. He's in the first toilet at present. We need to stop people coming into the corridor. Do you have a screen or something similar that we can use as a barrier?'

Donna and Lucy looked at each other. Lucy shrugged her shoulders. Donna answered.

'I think there's one in the Function Room.'

'Great. Let's put it up swiftly. It should stop people making their way down the corridor. If the staff ask, by the way, we're still sticking to the accident story. Screening off the bar will help enforce that but not for much longer because the diners will doubtless wonder where the ambulance is once we tell them there's been an accident. Donna, you mentioned a Function Room. Could it be used for interviews?'

'Interviews?' Lucy sounded appalled.

'Yes. We need to speak to everyone and interview anyone who might be considered a suspect.' Harry cleared his throat. 'Everyone includes you both, the waitresses and kitchen staff.'

Harry turned to Donna.

'You have access everywhere. It would be perfectly natural to see you in the bar, the corridor, anywhere.'

'Me? You think I…' Donna stared in astonishment at Harry. Then she laughed out loud, before quickly putting her hand in front of her mouth to shut down the sound.

Harry saw a flash of the sense of fun which was Donna's usual style.

'Why would I murder a customer? Come on, Harry, our income would soon vanish if I took to doing that.'

'Donna!' said Lucy.

'It's okay, Lucy. I can't imagine Donna killing anyone. She's more likely to laugh herself out of a murderous thought. I had to say that because everyone and anyone who's been in the corridor is going to be a suspect until we can clear them.'

'You'll have to cross me off your list, Harry,' said Lucy, 'because I've been in the kitchen all evening, as has Vi. We never left, at least not until Donna called me out to see you.'

'Thanks Lucy. That's exactly what I need to know. Who else is in the kitchen? The waitresses? I expect they will confirm what you said.'

'Agnes and Elsie, and Vi, who's the sous-chef.'

The door to the kitchen opened a crack. Harry stepped back to check out the eye that appeared in the gap.

'I bet that's Agnes,' said Donna. The door closed silently. 'Good luck questioning her, Agnes is a tough nut to crack.'

'Don't worry. We can be tough too. Before we move on, has anyone left the restaurant since the body was discovered?'

'No,' said Donna.

'Are you certain about that?'

Agnes came out of the kitchen door. 'The couple at table 6 want to pay and leave. Will you see to that, Donna?'

'Yes, in a moment.' Agnes stayed where she was. 'That's okay, Agnes, I'll organise the bill for them.'

Agnes slid back through the door, looking over her shoulder at Harry and Bradley.

When she was gone, Harry spoke. 'Didn't we agree that the staff would not use this door?'

'We did. Agnes doesn't like being told what to do.'

'Hmm. Okay Donna, I'll speak to Agnes. Let's sort the screen first, though. Bradley, will you go with Donna? Lucy, do you have a floorplan of the main room? Are the tables numbered?'

'We have a plan we use to note bookings and orders. Will that do?'

'Yes. May I have a copy of it please?'

Lucy went into the kitchen. Donna and Bradley went through the fire exit door in the bar which led to the Function Room. They soon returned, carrying an ornate wooden screen. It was clearly heavy. Harry grabbed the end Donna was holding. The screen was made of three panels of carved wood. They moved it carefully through the bar and stood it up in the corridor. Harry saw that the panels moved independently.

'Perfect,' he said. 'Can we put a couple of chairs behind it in case the screen falls over? We can leave an end panel clear and use that to give us access up and down the corridor.'

They placed the screen on the restaurant side of the toilet entrance.

Harry turned to Bradley. 'I'll speak to Lucy, Donna, Agnes and the other staff now.' He looked at his watch. 'The Ely PCs are taking their time. How close were you to finishing checks in the toilets?'

'The ones nearest the restaurant were almost done.'

'Okay. Stay here while I speak to the staff. If Oog comes out, ask him to go to the disabled toilet unless he has something to report.'

9

Sara felt ill. Murder? Someone nearby was a killer. There was a tightness in her chest.

Oog was gone from her side. He had been a barrier against the room. Now she and Charlotte were alone. What did Charlotte know of the world of crime? Sara had been around Harry for a long time. She was familiar with the phone ringing at odd hours, and also with piecing together drips of information to discover what was happening.

She must stay alert, keep her eyes open, be ready to notice anything odd or dangerous. Her skin prickled.

Charlotte was fiddling with her cutlery. 'They're slow clearing the plates,' she said.

Sara looked around the room again, slowly, carefully, trying to be unobtrusive.

To her right, on the far side of the open wooden panelling, three people sat at a round table. They were chatting happily.

Feeling like a spy, Sara listened in.

'He'll be back any day now,' said a woman. 'I can't

believe three months have gone by.'

An elderly man replied. 'He'll be changed.'

Laughter from the woman. 'Hopefully for the better!'

The conversation sounded fairly normal, but – how could Sara tell? Probably normal, she decided because she hadn't seen those people moving around.

Beyond that table, a settle ran along the end wall of the restaurant. It must have been a church pew, Sara thought, because she'd never seen a settle that long. It worked in the restaurant. Two tables, one for six diners, and a smaller one for four, were set at either end of the settle. A gap had been left between the tables to allow people to come and go.

Sara focussed on the nearer table. She couldn't hear what those people there were saying. The diners there were all of a similar age. They were jolly and totally engaged with each other and she hadn't seen them leave their table either.

Sara's roving eye moved to the table next to them, set for six. Her eyes met the angry glare of the man in the corner by the window. Oh dear, he must have noticed her looking around. Sara dropped her gaze.

She became aware that Charlotte was talking to her.

'Where are they gone? What's going on? Harry whispered something to you. What did he say?'

Sara had learnt over the years she'd been going out with Harry, never to comment on cases he was involved in. So the half-truth sprang easily to her lips. 'He said he was sorry to abandon me, us. I guess they're busy with the person who had the accident.'

'Have they called an ambulance? It's all very strange.'

'Yes, Charlotte, it is very strange.'

'May I ask you a personal question?'

What? Sara didn't like being asked personal questions.

'Eh, umm, well I guess so.'

She and Charlotte were on an evening out. This was the first time she had met Bradley's new girlfriend. Goodness, she hoped Charlotte wouldn't ask about Bradley's former girlfriends. Because he'd had a lot. Tall and with natural blond hair, he was very good-looking.

'Bradley hasn't mentioned you before. I didn't realise Harry had a girlfriend. He's joined us a couple of times in the pub and when we went to the theatre last week. Why haven't I met you before?'

As Sara considered her answer, the man from the end table by the window walked by. He looked down at her as he passed. Although slim, he had broad shoulders.

Oh no, he was heading down the corridor!

'What's going on?' asked Charlotte, whom Sara had momentarily forgotten.

'Oh, sorry, the, the…'

Sara overheard voices coming from the corridor. The man returned. He bustled back to his table, eyebrows drawn down sharply over his eyes. His girlfriend, or anyway the woman sitting opposite him, looked around. She spotted Sara, and looked away instantly. But in that small glance, Sara saw that the woman was as angry as the man. Her stare was intense. It was directed at the man, but it made Sara shiver.

'Sara?'

She looked back at Charlotte. What had she asked? Oh well, honesty was often the best policy.

'Sorry, Charlotte. I was about to say that Harry and I were together for a long time but we split up about a year ago.'

'Why?'

Sara didn't feel like talking about Harry and herself. After all, she'd only just met Charlotte. She took a breath. 'It's history.'

Charlotte didn't seem happy with that reply. 'I'm going to have a look at the bar,' she said, reaching down for her handbag.

Sara leaned close. 'You can't go down the corridor. The accident happened in the bar, I think. They're not letting anyone go there. Did you see the man who just passed? He was turned back.'

'I hate mysteries,' said Charlotte, sitting back down. 'And I don't like being close to the scene of a crime.'

Oops, thought Sara. She wondered how long Bradley and Charlotte would last as a couple.

10

When Harry entered the kitchen, he found five people standing around the central worktable.

'We want to know what's going on,' said Agnes, 'but Lucy and Donna won't tell us. We know something has happened. If someone's ill, like, where's the ambulance?'

Agnes was the one who'd been trying to push her nose into the investigation all evening. Had Donna said she was difficult?

'I am Detective Inspector Meredith from the Cambridgeshire Police. It's coincidental that I'm here this evening with my colleague, Detective Sergeant West. A third policeman is working with us. His name is Hugues Dubois. I am in charge. What I'm about to tell you has to remain confidential for the present. I need your assurance on that before I continue.'

Harry looked at everyone, slowly, eye to eye. They nodded one by one.

'I need all your names, apart from Lucy and Donna, whom I already know.'

Harry pulled out his notebook. Like the disposable

gloves, he carried it everywhere.

'Agnes Leonard,' chirped up Agnes before he'd set pen to paper.

He turned to a slim girl whose hair was pulled back completely from her face.

'Eh, Vi, Vi Marshall.'

Making a note, Harry turned to the last woman. He'd noticed her fidgeting while he was speaking. Her colour wasn't good. Perhaps she was squeamish. When she didn't speak, Harry looked across at Donna.

'This is Elsie Clay. She comes in at weekends.'

Why was Elsie Clay so nervous? Harry put an asterisk by her name.

'Thank you.' Harry paused before breaking the news to them. 'A person was seriously injured in the bar this evening. We're waiting for an ambulance.'

Elsie dropped a fork she'd been holding. Vi gasped. Agnes seemed to take the news in her stride.

'I can do first aid.'

'Thank you Agnes. That won't be necessary. We're all trained in that.'

'Whose looking after the poor woman?'

Harry wondered how Agnes knew it was a woman. He would ask later, rather than draw attention to it now. 'You don't need to worry about that.'

Harry looked at Agnes, Vi and Elsie. 'You won't be able to return to the dining rooms at present. My colleague, DS West and I will let the diners know what has happened. No one can leave the premises until we can clear them of involvement. Be aware that we will be taking statements from you soon.'

'What?' said Vi. 'I've never done a statement. I don't know how.'

'That's no problem. We'll ask a few questions and your

statement will be the answers to those questions.'

Harry looked around. 'Are there any chairs here?'

'No,' said Lucy. 'It's a working area.'

'It will take a while to work through people's details and statements and you might like to sit while you wait. I'll ask DS West to bring more chairs in from the Function Room. We have set up a screen blocking access to the bar.'

'Oh,' said Agnes. 'Oh.' She turned to Donna. 'Don't forget that the couple by the fire want their bill.'

Harry went back to the corridor and nodded to Bradley, who was waiting. They ducked inside the bar, leaving the curtain a little open as Harry kept an eye on the corridor. But before they could catch up, a man pushed through the screen. He was unsteady on his feet.

'So wherz Geoff Norman?' he asked. 'Duzee know where N'tasha is? She wen' to toilet but hasn't come back and the women are giving me stick. But 'snot my fault.'

11

Sara noticed a man coming out of the Victorian Room. He was unsteady on his feet. He seemed to fall into the corridor. She jumped up to follow him, but when she got to the corridor, she found a screen blocking the way. It was no barrier to the small, thin man. He pushed a section open and kept going. The screen wobbled. Sara was afraid it was going to topple over, but it held steady.

She stepped through after the man.

Sara had to stop abruptly as he was standing by an alcove leading to toilets. 'N'tasha?' he called, knocking at one door.

He waited briefly, then tapped on the second door and called again.

Oog emerged from the second toilet. He was wearing disposable gloves.

Harry came towards them. He stopped, frowned at Sara, then moved to stand beside the man. 'What are you doing here?'

'So wherz Geoff Norman? Duzee know where N'tasha is? She wen' to toilet but hasn't come back and the wimen wanna know where she iz.'

Harry looked from Sara to the man. 'Who are you looking for?'

'Whassit to you?' The man fell back again the wall.

He hit his head hard. Sara winced.

'Did you say Natasha?' asked Harry.

'M… m… girlfriend?'

Definitely tipsy, thought Sara. Anaesthetised. He hadn't even reacted when he banged his head.

'Whassit to you?' He said again, sounding aggressive.

Why couldn't Harry take the man into a side room?

Sara inched further down the corridor, wanting to know more. The door to her left opened a couple of inches. Sara saw an eye in the gap. Food smells floated out. That must be the kitchen.

A noise made her glance back. The man was sliding down the wall. Harry pushed him upright again.

Donna came through the screen from the restaurant.

The eye in the gap disappeared and the kitchen door closed quietly.

'Do you know this man, Donna?' asked Harry.

'No, but I think he's with Geoff Norman's group.'

'Whaz going on?' asked the man.

Donna rolled her eyes. 'I've checked all the tables. The only gaps are in the Victorian Room. Three gaps. One will be Geoff, another this man and…'

Donna noticed Sara. She tried to smile but Sara saw the smile fade. Donna went into the kitchen. The lovely blast of food smells seemed at odds with what was happening.

Harry checked his watch. 'How long has your girlfriend been missing from the table?'

'A… 'bout five minz.'

The only person Sara had seen go down the corridor and not return, had been the woman. Donna had accompanied the laughing man, the one who was now standing by the front door. Sara looked in that direction. She saw through the open panel of the screen that he was still there, and staring down at them. If this drunken man was from the other dining room and Harry needed to know who he was, then wouldn't it be useful to ask the man from the door to join them?

'It must have been a lot more than five minutes ago, Mr...?

'Anstey. FrAnstey.'

Sara felt out of her depth. What sort of a name was that?

'Mr Anstey. How come you haven't noticed your girlfriend's absence before now?'

'Been buzy, talk to friends. Don't see 'em mush now. Chrizmas party... She was, was talkin' to women. Need her to drive me home.'

'How sober are you, Mr Anstey?'

'I'm not driving! N'tasha will.'

Bradley came through the curtain at the end of the corridor.

She must be in there. The woman. Sara felt sick.

'*Excusez moi*, Sara.' Oog must have been standing behind her and she hadn't noticed. Sara jumped. He slid past her through a door with a disabled toilet sign.

What was he doing in there? Searching for evidence, if the disposable gloves were anything to go by.

'Bradley, will you take Mr Anstey back to the Victorian Room? We really need a guard to stop people coming through that screen.'

Harry turned to her. 'Sara, go back to your table, please. I'll be out in a moment.'

As she turned the corner of the corridor, Sara saw that the man sitting beside them at the table by the end of the corridor, whom Harry had called Tom, was staring at her.

'What is going on?' he asked. 'I keep hearing noises.'

Bradley appeared behind her. 'Please take your seat, sir. We'll be along in a moment to explain.'

Bradley had a firm hold of Mr Anstey's arm, but the man waved his free arm and shouted. 'Geoffgeoff!' at the man guarding the front door.

Geoff stepped forward but Bradley shook his head and waved him back. He manoeuvred Mr Anstey into the other dining room.

Heavens, this was turning into the of strangest of evenings.

Sara sat back at her table.

'Where did Bradley go? Why hasn't he come back?'

Charlotte looked close to tears. Sara put an arm around her.

'Something bad has happened, hasn't it?' said Charlotte.

Sara rubbed the girl's arm and shrugged her shoulders. She looked around the room again. The noise levels had dropped. People were turning to look at her. Harry and Bradley should make an announcement about what had happened, and soon.

Donna appeared, carrying a small black folder. She laid it on the table by the fire.

'What's happening, Donna?' asked the man who was sitting there.

'Give me two minutes.' She dashed away.

Sara became aware of whisperings. Tom from the next table stood up and moved to the start of the corridor.

Harry appeared. 'I'm sorry, Tom, but you can't go down there.' The man backed away from him.

Harry and Bradley exchanged a glance. Bradley was standing by the coat hooks. They nodded to each other.

Bradley stepped into the other room.

'Excuse me,' said Harry as he stood by the dresser. He raised his voice. 'Excuse me,' he said again. The whisperings stopped. 'May I have your attention, please?'

12

'I am Inspector Meredith from the Cambridgeshire Police. I happened to be here for dinner this evening. A serious incident has occurred,' he said.

As Harry watched, a couple of people stood up. Shrieks and high-pitched talking filled the room. An echo of the same reaction sounded from the Victorian Room. Bradley was breaking the news in there.

Harry didn't want to mention murder. Panic would be difficult to contain with such a small investigative team. Where were the Ely crew?

'Would you all remain at your tables for the present, please? We will come to talk to you as quickly as we can.'

By his estimate, Harry thought there must be at least fifty diners in the restaurant. It was full to capacity. The shock of something of this nature intruding on their seasonal enjoyment would sober the customers. Many would want to leave and this was where he and his team would encounter problems. They had to contain everyone until it was possible to whittle down the suspect list. Suspect list? So far they had no suspects, or rather all too many possible suspects.

He, Bradley and Oog must work quickly to get names and addresses.

As Harry glanced around the room, his gaze lingered on his own table. He, Sara and Oog had had prime views of the entrance to the corridor. But Harry had been so intent on engaging with Sara that he had taken almost no notice of what was going on around them.

Oog, as far as he could remember had been focussed on his food and Sara.

Bradley and Charlotte had been engrossed in each other. And their backs had been to the corridor.

Sara. She probably had the best view in the entire room. What might she have seen?

He knew she was a keen observer. As a lecturer, she was used to gauging behaviour and reactions. She was a good teacher, mostly because she thought about her students and noticed them. He would speak to her before they started going around from table to table.

She was standing behind her chair, in the corner of the wooden partition, observing the room. Harry met her eye as it travelled back to him. She gave him a slight nod.

Harry thanked his lucky stars that, although they had ended their relationship, she had never been difficult or resentful. Sara had an unusual degree of maturity.

He realised her nod meant she had something to tell him. Harry jerked his head towards the corridor. Sara followed him. He pushed open the screen panel.

It was dark in the corridor with the screen cutting off light from the Oak Room, and the curtain sealing off the bar. There were wall lights but the light they gave was low. Harry reached out a hand to take Sara's. He squeezed, she squeezed back. They dropped their hands.

'I'm wondering if you noticed anyone moving around

this evening, leaving their table, going down the corridor?'

'I did, several people in fact. That's what I wanted to tell you. I saw a woman coming out of the room behind the fireplace – the other dining room? She's the woman who's been killed, isn't she?'

'Yes,' said Harry, flipping open his notebook and holding back his impression of Natasha Poole's similarity to Sara's mother. 'Did anyone else come out of that room?'

'The chap who's guarding the front door now, and a small thin man came out but that was much later, and you spoke to him just now.'

'Yes. Anyone else move about?'

'A man from the table beside us went down the corridor at the same time as the woman. The older man, oiled back dark hair, tall? I think you called him Tom.'

'Yes. Tom Black.'

'Well Mr Black returned, but the woman didn't. I also saw a young man from the table opposite us, by the window, the table for two, walk down. Actually, he ran. He'd been getting lots of messages on his phone and his companion wasn't happy about that. He came back fairly quickly. Also, a couple right at the end of the room, the table for six by the window. They both left their table. I'm sure the man left first, then the woman who'd been sitting opposite him. And they were having a row of sorts too, though it was a silent row. They stopped talking to the others at their table. I think that's all I noticed.'

'Thank you, Sara. That's really helpful. How certain are you of what you saw?'

'I'm fairly sure that what I saw is accurate. I'm used to classrooms and lecture halls. There's always a student who tries to slide out. I'm sure I noticed everyone from the main room, the Oak Room, leave and return. I can't swear to what happened in the far room. Anyone could have come out past the dresser when I was looking elsewhere and I wouldn't have seen them.'

'And yet you noticed Mr Anstey. The drunken man,' he added.

'Oh, yes. Well he was impossible to miss. He wobbled so much I was sure he'd fall over.'

'Great. Will you go back to your seat now?'

Harry went to the bar and wrote down what Sara had said on his copy of the floor plan. He put initials by his own party at the big round table.

The table for four next to his was where Tom Black and his group were sitting. Table 15. Harry noted TB+3 on that. No matter what good press Tom Black was given, no matter that Harry had met him and that the Red Lion knew him well, he had to go on Harry's suspect list.

Also on that list were the couple sitting at the small round table opposite Harry's own party. He marked that table with a Mars and Venus sign, and ringed Mars for the man Sara had seen go down the corridor with his phone. A second suspect.

Harry marked the 6+ by the end table on the window side of the room, table 10, and again put in the planet symbols against the man and woman, and ringed them. Another two added to the list.

That gave him four possible suspects.

Harry added Fred Anstey, the drunken man from the ex-Young Farmers party. He was the person who had brought Natasha Poole to the Red Lion. That increased the number of suspects to five.

Once they began questioning the diners, they could end up with more suspects. People were good at noticing was happened close to them.

Harry added the staff to his list as they would also need to be considered. Indeed the staff had more opportunity than anyone as they had been moving freely through in and out of the rooms, and up and down the corridor. Agnes, Elsie and Vi. He was sure most if not all of them would be removed from the list, but they had to go on until they could be eliminated. That gave him a total of 8 suspects, as things stood. He would like someone else to corroborate Sara's observations.

Harry thought briefly of a novel he had once read. It was by Agatha Christie, about a murder which took place on an island off the coast of Devon. There had been a large number of suspects in that case. He even remembered the title of the book: *And Then There Were None.* Harry wasn't likely to end up with no suspects. A woman had been murdered and he needed to find her killer. He would whittle his list down. He had the possible 'Who' and he knew the when and where. What eluded him at present was the 'Why'? Why had someone killed Natasha Poole?

13

There was bound to be trouble when the diners realised they were locked in.

It soon came.

The young man at the small table for two, table 8, who was on Harry's list, jumped up. He pushed past Harry and headed for the restaurant door. Geoff Norman had left his post to listen to Harry talking. He was unprepared for the onslaught.

'Stop!' cried Harry, leaping after the man.

He caught him as the man began to pull on the door handle. Harry felt a painful wrench in his bad arm.

'It won't open!' shouted the man. 'Let me out!'

Brilliant. Now everyone knew they were locked in.

Harry pulled the young man away from the door. Bradley came out of the Victorian Room and helped restrain him.

Why had he tried to run?

And where could they take him to ask that question?

'You have to let me go,' shouted the man. 'You can't hold me here against my will. I've done nothing.'

Every pair of eyes was on them. If Harry didn't contain this situation, more people might rush to leave. They would not be able to hold them all back.

Help came in the shape of Donna.

She addressed the room. 'Everyone,' she said, 'Lucy and I would be grateful if you would work with Inspector Meredith. I will be coming from table to table shortly to sort out bills and the Inspector and his team will want to know if you have any information to give us.'

Harry turned to Donna and nodded. Thank goodness she had such good rapport with the customers. The diners were whispering, looking at each other, looking daggers at Harry, but they were staying at their tables.

Behind him, people began to emerge from the Victorian Room. They pushed past Bradley who had backed towards the corridor, still restraining the man who'd tried to leave.

There were shouts of 'What's going on? What's happening?'

Harry spoke to the group who had clustered by the entrance to the Victorian Room. 'Please move further into the room.'

It would be better to talk to everyone together.

Two women at the head of the group eyed Harry. Geoff came over to them. 'It's okay. We should do as the Inspector asks.'

The group dribbled into gaps between the tables.

Harry gestured to Bradley to take his charge into the now empty Victorian Room. They could question the young man there.

Geoff was sent back to his post by the front door. A few of the group huddled by him. Harry hoped Geoff wouldn't let them leave. What a mess.

'Wherz N'tasha?' It was Mr Anstey again.

'Will you go and stand by Geoff, please.'

Harry stood on the raised step at the end of the corridor. He heard the whispers repeating the dead woman's name. Things were getting a bit chaotic.

At the sound of a faint squeak, Harry turned and saw Oog was pushing the screen open. He held up an evidence bag briefly, putting it swiftly behind his back. Harry gave Oog a thumbs up.

Harry moved back into the Oak Room. 'Everyone,' he called out. 'Listen.' The murmurings continued. Harry raised his voice. 'LISTEN!'

That quieted them.

'We will be speaking to everyone, but for the present I need you all to be calm and to remain here in the main room. We will work as swiftly as possible and let you leave as soon as we can. Please help by remaining where you are. There is no threat to you. We simply need your patience and compliance. Is that clear?'

There were a lot of mumblings and a few 'yes sirs'.

Soon people would wonder why they were being contained if what had happened was simply an accident.

Tom Black hovered near Harry. He whispered. 'I got a good view of all the comings and goings. I might be able to help.'

'Thank you, Tom. I'll speak to you very soon.'

People were talking to each other, many hovering by Donna, whom they knew. Those who had come out of the Victorian Room were talking to Geoff Norman, who seemed to be calming them. At least they were listening.

He must speak to Oog.

Leaving Donna and Geoff to manage the Oak Room, Harry went swiftly down the corridor. He and Oog slipped into the bar.

'There is an old ceramic barrel,' said Oog. 'We have them

in France, for wines. The tap is no longer there, but I spotted something in the hole. I use the light from the torch and *voila*!' He lifted up the evidence bag in which rested the small black-handled knife Donna had described.

'Well done, Oog.'

Harry took the bag and locked it into the SoC box on the table.

'We have a situation here, Oog, and it's in danger of getting out of hand. Bradley is in the other dining room with a man who tried to get away. We need to question him. There is also a man who says the deceased is his girlfriend.'

'*Mais*,' said Oog, glancing at his watch.

'Indeed,' said Harry. 'Why didn't he miss her earlier? He wasn't paying attention to her, it seems. I want to talk to Geoff Norman, the man at the door who is part of that group. If he can remember who left the room, we may be able to eliminate some or all of the rest, apart from Natasha Poole's boyfriend.'

Lucy came into the bar. 'Harry, I've been thinking about extra space that you might use. We have an office upstairs, as I said. You could use that.'

'That is really helpful, Lucy. Thanks.'

Lucy left the bar.

'That is very good *n'est ce pas*? And now, what would you like me to do?'

'Now that you've found the murder weapon, I think we should keep this corridor space free. Will you stand at the far side of the screen and put off anyone attempting to enter? Seeing you there should be a deterrent. I will check if Bradley has had time to question our escapee. We need to move on swiftly with getting information, names, addresses and such.'

'*D'accord*.'

A shout came from down the corridor.

'Harry!'

14

Harry ran down to the Victorian Room. The man who'd tried to leave through the front door was now hammering on the French doors which led to a patio. Bradley was pulling him away. The doors were locked but the man was pushing against them firmly and they were shaking.

Harry took one arm and Bradley the other. They wrenched the man away from the doors.

If only they had handcuffs.

They pushed the young man onto a chair at the end of the room.

'What is your name and why are you trying to escape?' asked Harry.

The man was almost in tears. 'It's, it's em, uh, ah…Casey. Don Casey. I have to get out of here. My wife can't know I've been out with Rochelle again. I promised.' He laid his head on the table and whimpered. 'We're expecting a baby. She's threatened to throw me out if I ever saw Rochelle again.'

'Mr Casey, I'm cautioning you not to leave this chair until I can speak to the girl you mention. Rochelle? Which table is she at?'

'The second table, by the window. It was just us two.'

The man's nose was running. Harry picked up a napkin from the table and passed it to him. 'If you move we'll arrest you,' he said, firmly. 'Have you got that?'

The man sniffed loudly, then blew into the napkin. 'Yeah.'

Harry went back to the main room. He saw a worried-looking young woman sitting alone at a table for two, beside a window fronting onto the road.

'Rochelle?' he asked as he walked up to the table.

'What's happened to Johnny?'

Johnny?

'Come with me please?'

The chair squeaked as Rochelle pushed it back.

Harry led her to the screen in the corridor. Behind him, he heard a surge of whispering and low voices. How much longer would they manage to contain the diners?

'Rochelle, is it?'

'Yeah.'

'Follow me upstairs, please.'

'Where's Johnny?' She called after him.

Harry stopped near the top. 'Up,' he pointed.

Rochelle was pouting. She flipped her long hair over her shoulder and sashayed past him. Harry led the way into the office.

He drew out a chair but Rochelle refused to sit.

'What have you done to Johnny?' Her arms crossed her thin body. She wobbled a bit. Whether from alcohol or fear, Harry couldn't say, but he knew she would be frightened as well as angry.

'Don Casey is downstairs talking to my colleague.'

'Casey?' she repeated, looking puzzled.

Ah, a false surname. 'Did I get that wrong?'

'Yeah, you did! His name is Johnny Rouse. JR.'

As soon as she said the name, Rochelle began to blush.

'Don Casey, or JR, or Johnny Rouse, which is it?' said Harry, not turning a hair.

Rochelle continued to stand.

Harry waited.

Rochelle began to chew her inner cheek.

'Okay Rochelle, did Mr Rouse leave the table during your meal? Please tell me the truth. I will discover it sooner or later, but it will make things easier for you and Mr Rouse if you tell me now.'

'He never did. But, but… then maybe he had to go to the toilet. He drinks beer. Makes you pee a lot. But he stayed sitting with me the whole evening. He never did nothing.'

'So he left the table, you say.'

'Yeah yeah. It's so hard for him. We want to be together but that bitch wife of his got herself pregnant.' Rochelle shook herself, walked over to the window.

Harry sighed. Another small tragedy. But at least Rochelle and Mr Rouse were alive, unlike Natasha Poole.

'Did you leave the table at any point?'

'No, I didn't,' she began to sniff. 'Like honest I didn't. It's our last night out before, before… I didn't want to miss a minute of being with Johnny.' Loud sniff.

'Okay Rochelle. Thank you. I want you to go back downstairs and return to your table. Don't talk to anybody. Do you understand?'

'But, but what about Johnny? Will he be coming back to the table too?'

'In a while.'

Harry gestured at the stairs. Rochelle didn't move. He looked at her. She rolled her eyes, tossed her hair, sniffed, then moved.

When they reached the bottom, Harry watched as she returned to her table. She looked over her shoulder at him. He gave her a good hard stare. Rochelle sat in Johnny's vacant seat rather than her own. She sniffed again. This time Harry watched tears roll down her cheeks. He turned away. Perhaps taking Johnny Rouse's seat gave her some comfort. She might need it as the evening wore on.

'Inspector, can we have that word?' Tom Black was at Harry's side. He lowered his voice. 'The man who tried to get out? I know him. His name is Johnny Rouse. He delivers to my yard. I noticed him earlier.'

'Thank you, Tom. Come with me.'

Harry led the way back upstairs. He took out his notebook.

'My table is at the bottom of the corridor. I saw who went up and down. I have prostate trouble and I went to the toilet. I saw Johnny Rouse go down towards the bar.'

'That's interesting, Tom.' Harry took out his notebook and began writing. 'Did you notice anyone else go along the corridor?'

'I did. Rousie first, then Paul Leonard and his wife – they're sitting on the end table, the one by the window. Then one of the waitresses, Agnes… I don't know the other one. Then Donna, and a woman, a different woman. I know her. Natasha Poole. They all came back to their seats, but Natasha didn't.'

Harry noted everything. He would compare this to what Sara had noticed. It seemed the same.

'Will you return to your seat for the present, Tom? We'll take a full statement from you later.'

'Sure.'

Harry looked at his floorplan when Tom Black left. He wrote initials for people who'd been in the corridor, including the staff, and even Sara. There had been a lot of traffic in the area.

Lucy and Donna were waiting for him when he descended the stairs.

'Harry, Lucy and I would like to talk to you.'

'Shall we go down the corridor or upstairs?'

'The corridor. This won't take long.'

Harry hoped the screen panel was robust. It was certainly getting a lot of action.

'We've decided not to charge people for their meals,' said Lucy.

Harry raised his eyebrows. 'Really? That's a generous gesture.'

'We like our customers and we want them to return. Hopefully the free meal will soften the shock of what's happened.'

'That is smart thinking, Lucy. I won't try to dissuade you. I'm certain it will be much appreciated by your customers.'

'We hope so. Many will have had their evenings spoiled but,' Lucy stopped, towards the curtained-off bar, 'of course it's a minor thing when I think of that poor woman. I hope they'll all understand when they find out the truth.'

'We will hope so. Now, Bradley and I are planning to go from table to table asking if anyone has seen anything. We must get names and addresses so that we can contact people later, if needed. While we're standing here, it occurs to me that it would be better if you spoke to the customers ahead of us. I think it would oil our path.'

'Sure,' said Lucy. 'And we can ask them to be helpful to you. Okay Donna?

Donna nodded.

'Before that, I plan to hold a witness in the Function Room – the man who tried to escape.'

Donna and Lucy gasped and spoke in tandem. 'The killer?'

'I can't say at the moment. We need a private space to hold him in.'

Lucy and Donna looked at each other. They were a good team. 'Why not hold him upstairs? Then you can usher the Young Farmers back to the Victorian Room, and the Function Room can be an extra space.'

'That will help enormously. We will need a second space in which to interview people. I'm hoping the Ely police will arrive shortly. They can take over guard duties.' Harry looked at his watch. 'I don't know what's keeping them.'

Donna looked at Lucy, then spoke to Harry. 'It might be easier for customers if I check names and addresses. I know most of them, apart from the group booking, but Geoff Norman knows them. It's his party. He could get the details for us.'

'Thank you, Lucy, Donna. I'm very grateful to you for this help, especially in these difficult circumstances. You're marvellous.' Harry turned to go then stopped. 'I'm just wondering what might speed things up. Do you mind if Sara Engemann, from our table, goes with you? She can jot down the details of names and addresses as you ask for them.'

'That will be fine.'

'Okay. I'll let Bradley and Oog know what we're doing, then I will to speak to Sara. It will have to be in the corridor, I guess. The sooner we can let people go the better. Are there spare keys to the Function Room in case it needs to be locked?'

'I'll get you a set,' said Donna.

* * * * *

Back in the Victorian Room, Johnny Rouse was still

snivelling. He raised his head as Harry came in. His eyes were red and bloodshot.

'Mr Rouse.'

The man sunk his head back down on the table.

'Rouse? Not Casey?' asked Bradley.

'Yes, Mr Rouse has lied to us. Take a statement from him, Bradley. I'll get the blank witness statement forms from the SoC box.'

* * * * *

Having passed the forms to Bradley, Harry joined Oog at the end of the corridor and motioned him up the stairs. Harry filled him in and said they had to keep Johnny Rouse under guard.

'Harry, we need more people. There is not enough to do all the jobs.'

'I know. It's a problem. I'm going to involve Sara. She can help.'

'Harry, you must not put Sara in danger.'

'She won't be in danger. I will ask her to do admin stuff. I think Charlotte could be drafted in too. She can help Sara take down names and addresses. It will be better for her to have something to do.'

'And who will be on guard?'

'I was getting to that. The policing logistics aren't good, I know. Geoff Norman is on the front door. I'd like you to stay with Johnny Rouse.'

'And this Mr Rouse, you think he is the killer?'

'I don't know, but we can't let him return to the Oak Room.'

'*Mais non*, but we should handcuff him to stop him trying to leave again.'

'Unfortunately, we don’t have cuffs in the SoC box and

neither Bradley nor I came dressed for crime.'

'I have cuffs.'

'You do?'

'Yes, I come close to many bad people. I am always prepared.' Hugues drew a set of cuffs from the depths of a trouser pocket. They were packed in a plastic case. It would have disguised them and prevented them from rattling.

Harry beamed. 'Nice one, Oog. Let's cuff Mr Rouse.'

15

WITNESS STATEMENT

Statement of: *johnny rouse*
Age if under 18: *I am over 18*
Occupation: *agricultral deliverer*

This statement (consisting of 3 page(s) each signed by me) is true to the best of my knowledge and belief and I make it knowing that, if it is tendered in evidence, I shall be liable to prosecution if I have wilfully stated in it anything which I know to be false, or do not believe to be true.

Witness Signature: *jrouse* Date: *07/12/2024*

I am the above name person, I come here this, evening with my girlfriend. her name is rochelle, goodge Shes not my wife. My wife doessnt know Im' here. Is the last time Im' going to see rochelle I swear. Shes getting pushy but my wife is pregnant and I have to stop seeing rochelle or my wife says she will kick me out.

I did not leave my table all evening until I tried to get out of here, I did not know the door, was locked, That wassnt right. We shoudnt not be locked in, Ive' done nothing. Neither has Rochelle. Is costing me a lot of money, to take her for dinner here at the red line, I only brought her here because I had to tell her we cant meet again and I heard the food is really good and that was a bonus cos she might not be so angry about breaking up after a good meal.

So we got here around 7, The place wassnt really full but Id booked a table for two cos Id looked in the window and saw it was all posh. Lots more people came in after that. See I did not, want anyone else at our table because I needed to speak to her Rochelle with out anyone listening private like. I made sure no one I knew was around us. If there had been we woud have had to leave. But I knew no one cep't for tom black who I deliver to. tom black is a good sort. He always helps us out. I remember he was kind to natasher. Im' sure he will stand up for me and give me a good, reference like. But anyways we ordered our food, I got white wine for Rochelle. I don't drink wine, I had a beer, I kept filling up her glass to put her in a good mood.

She hates my wife rochelle does.

My wife is pregnant.

I have to be let go from here you cant keep me. The baby is due any day, I have to be with Tracy for the birth she says and afterwards too. She cant know that I've been seeing rochelle again. Well she does know but I said it was over. Tracy said I woudnt not get near the baby if I did not stop seeing her Rochelle. I cant have that Is my baby too. So rochelle has to go.

I lied about my name, Is not don casey that name belongs to a friend. I was frightened the police woud tell my wife and then I wouldn't not get to see the baby. My wife might even throw me out of the house. I was only trying to stop. the worst happening. my real name is johnny rouse.

I never left the table I was trying to soften rochelle up. She can be hard and angry. I only did not want her to be angry because then she might not break up with me and I cant change my phone number because the wife will want to know why and I have to be available.

So when the other policeman said there had been an accident I just had to leave. I did not want truble or my name in the paper. My wife woud know Id been lying to her. I told her I was going to meet my mate charlee for a few beers.

I did not not leave my table all evening I did not not even go for a pee, I only drunk some of my beer I was trying to stay sober. It wassnt me who caused any accident. I know nothing about any accident.

Note by DS Bradley West:
We are using blank witness forms from the SOC box and asking witnesses to write their statements out by hand. They have been made aware that the written statements will be printed up when we get back to the Cambridge Police Station.

16

'I can't tell what's happening from here,' said Agnes, who had pushed open a gap in the *Out* door leading to the rear of the Oak Room. 'When that detective person's back is turned I'm going to talk to my cousin. He should know what's going on. It's not right keeping us locked here in the kitchen. It's just mean.'

'Oh don't do it, Agnes. We'll get into trouble.'

'Shut up, Elsie. You're such a wimp.'

'Lucy and Donna will be cross if you go out to the Oak Room, Agnes.'

'I don't care. I'm doing it. Whistle if you see the detective coming back.'

Agnes dropped to the floor and scuttled across to her cousin's table.

Mrs Gotobed was nearest to her. She tugged at the woman's leg to announce her arrival. Jane Gotobed screamed.

'Oh shut up you stupid cow,' hissed Agnes. 'Now everyone will notice I'm here.'

'Have you come to take the dessert order?' asked Ida

Manners.

'Paul, Paul,' whispered Agnes. She frog-hopped to his chair by the window.

'What are you doing, Aggie? You could get caught.' said Paul. 'Do you know what's going on?'

"The police are out in the corridor or in the Victorian Room or prancing about upstairs in the office. They're not going to notice. Tell me what's happening here?'

Paul didn't seem his usual fun self. He looked peaky and red around the eyes. Had he been crying? What did he have to cry about? When they were children they often played tricks on the grown-ups and Paul had been great fun back then. Agnes hadn't seen him in a while. He always seemed to be out somewhere when she called to his home.

'Like, what's going on Paul? What have the police said to you?'

'Get back to the kitchen,' said Paul's wife Kylie, crossly. 'You were always getting Paul into trouble. Go away. Don't talk to her, Paul. She'll only make things worse.'

Agnes saw her cousin's face go white. Was he that scared of his wife?

'Go away,' said Kylie again. 'If you don't, I'll call the policeman and tell him you're there.'

Agnes stared up at Kylie, narrowing her eyes. 'I'll get you. Just you wait.'

She crouched back down, slid slowly past Kylie's legs, pinched her, grinned when Kylie said *ouch*, and hopped swiftly back to the kitchen.

Elsie, who'd been watching stood back from the door as Agnes barged in. 'You shouldn't have done that, Agnes. There'll be trouble. What if those people tell the police? And that Mrs Manners, she's trouble.'

Agnes rolled her eyes. 'Maybe you all think it's fine to

be stuck here in the kitchen where we can't even sit down while that lot are out there eating and drinking and the police are running around like they own the place, but I don't!'

'The diners must have run out of drink by now,' said Vi. 'And food. I wonder if you should clear the tables? It would give you something to do.'

Agnes narrowed her eyes but she held her tongue. Vi had been working at the Red Lion longer than her and…

'Oh don't get us into trouble,' whinged Elsie. 'My Mum will kill me if I get into trouble with the police. Can't you just behave?'

'You're a rabbit, Elsie Clay, a scaredy cat, a wimp. What are the police going to do to us? We haven't done anything wrong. We haven't murdered anyone. Have we?'

Elsie began to cry. 'No but, no… but I did… '

'Stop snivelling, Elsie.

'Stop being nasty, Agnes.' Vi moved to stand by Elsie. 'And leave Elsie alone. We're all in this together and we should stick together.'

Agnes crossed her arms on her chest and began growling. 'Don't you wonder what's going on, Vi? Like who's upstairs? Like who killed the woman in the bar? Like who– '

Lucy came into the kitchen from the corridor side. 'Where's the table plan? The master list?'

Agnes pointed to the noticeboard.

'Thank you, Agnes.' Lucy took the sheet. 'Donna and I are going around the tables. Will you finish clearing up here, please?'

'Elsie and I have cleared all we can,' said Vi. 'We need to start clearing the tables.'

'That will have to wait.'

'What about the bills?' asked Agnes.

'Donna and I have decided not to charge anyone.'

'What? But that means we won't get tips!' Agnes huffed and tapped her foot.

Lucy looked cross. Agnes turned away, picked up a cloth, began polishing a clean surface slowly. Lucy left the kitchen. Agnes threw the cloth away.

Elsie edged toward the door leading from the kitchen to the car park.

Vi checked the dishwasher.

17

Harry and Bradley stood by the unlit fireplace in the Victorian Room. Oog was guarding the now handcuffed Mr Rouse at the far end of the table. Harry was examining his annotated floorplan.

Keeping his voice low, Harry spoke. 'Sara gave me her list and Tom Black saw the same people coming and going down the corridor. That gives us four possible suspects, or five if we count Mr Anstey.'

'You're putting Tom Black down as a suspect?'

'Everyone's a suspect until we find the killer, Bradley, however unlikely that may seem. I've also put question marks by the staff, apart from Lucy, Vi and Donna. Lucy and Vi were in the kitchen all evening, and Donna was front of house and in full view.'

'It's a different landscape isn't it, investigating when we're in a social situation. I suppose we should also put ourselves on the list.'

'Very funny, Bradley. Let's focus on how we'll proceed. We've lost Oog because he's now guarding Mr Rouse. We need to reduce the number of people in the Oak Room.'

'We could lead the ex-Young Farmers' group back to the Victorian Room and ask Geoff Norman to keep an eye on them. Doesn't he know them?'

'It would be a good move but it would leave us without a guard on the front door. That's too dangerous. Mr Norman should be able to calm his group down. By the way, Lucy and Donna have decided not to charge the customers for their meals.'

'Nice move.'

'Yes. Lucy and Donna will go from table to table, explaining this. You and I will follow, to ask questions. Let's focus on the basics: Have you left your table this evening? Have you been to the bar? Have you visited the toilets? Have you noticed anyone in the corridor? Then, I would like Lucy and Donna to follow after us. Sara and hopefully Charlotte, will bring up the rear and take names and addresses. Once that's complete, most of the diners should be free to leave. We'll hang on to anyone who saw something useful. They'll need to give a statement. Our biggest problem will be where to hold people whom we consider suspicious.'

'What are our options, Harry?'

'The office upstairs and the Function Room are the only free spaces at present.'

Bradley had three sheets of paper in his hand.

'Is that Mr Rouse's statement?'

'Yes.'

Harry read it. 'He's lying about not leaving his table. Both Sara and Tom saw him go down the corridor. Let's take him upstairs and question him again.'

Harry signalled to Oog, who joined them. He filled Oog in. 'Try to get him upstairs with a minimum of fuss. We could screen him from view as we move him to the stairs. I don't want the diners to see the handcuffs. If Lucy and

Donna are still by the dresser, they'll help. Then I'll ask Geoff Norman to bring his group back here. I want to ask Lucy and Donna to make a start in this room. It will have to be a group chat because they were all sitting at this one big table.'

'*D'accord*, Harry.

Bradley went over to Mr Rouse. 'Stand up, we're moving you.'

'Where? I told you I haven't done anything.'

'What you've done, mate, is lie. We know you went down the corridor earlier.'

Rousie began to shake. 'I won't make trouble. Honest. I only went to the toilet to take a call from my wife. She was going mad. I couldn't take the call in the restaurant. Rochelle was sitting just across from me. And Tracy is loud. I only went there to have a bit of quiet. Honest. That's the truth. Ask Rochelle.'

Harry went back to the Oak Room. Lucy and Donna were by the dresser. He whispered that he was moving Mr Rouse upstairs. They agreed to help shield him from view. When he turned back to the Victorian Room, Bradley, Oog and a cowed Mr Rouse were waiting by the coats. Forming a line, they shooed Johnny Rouse to the bottom of the stairs. He climbed meekly, with Oog ahead of him and Bradley behind.

*****

Having overseen the Victorian Room diners back into their space, Harry nodded to Sara who joined himself, Lucy and Donna at the bottom of the stairs.

Harry nodded to Lucy and Donna. 'Bradley and I will speak to Geoff Norman's group first, and then go from table to table in the Oak Room. Would you follow us, saying that there will be no charge?'

'Sara, would you and Charlotte then take down names and addresses?'

'Sure, Harry.'

'Good. Donna, once you finish, I'd like you to stay on the front door instead of Geoff. Bradley and I will mark a floorplan with cleared tables and pass that to you. Anyone leaving should be checked against that list.'

Sara said she would check if Charlotte would join her in taking down names and addresses. 'I have a couple of notebooks in my bag.'

Harry smiled. Sara always carried a huge bag and, like Mary Poppins's bag, it had just about everything in it.

* * * * *

Now they were back in the Victorian Room, the ex-Young Farmers' group were milling about, all talking at once. A number were asking when Geoff was going to join them.

Harry spoke. 'Everyone, could you please resume your original seats. We will speak to you all individually. We will require your names and addresses. Detective Sergeant West will follow with a few questions about the evening, but first Lucy has something to say.'

The group sat down. Harry motioned Lucy to join him. It was the spot where sound would be most muffled. He didn't want people in the Oak Room to overhear.

Amid a lot of whispering, Lucy coughed. 'Hello everyone. Donna and I are sorry for the way the evening has turned out.'

'So what's happened?' asked a man by the window.

Harry stepped forward. 'There's been an accident.'

'Who was hurt?' asked the same man.

'Natasha's missing,' said a woman further down the

table. 'She was sitting here,' the woman said, pointing to an empty seat.

The room erupted as everyone began talking at once.

'Quiet,' called Harry. 'Let Lucy speak, and then DS West and I will talk to you and answer your questions as best as we can.'

Lucy told them that no charge would be made for their meals.

'What about the drinks,' asked someone. His speech was slurred.

'No charge at all,' said Lucy.

She and Donna left the room at a nod from Harry.

'Okay,' Harry took over. 'We have a series of questions. When we're finished, would you please give your name and address to Sara and Charlotte.' Harry pointed to the two women. They had notebooks and pens ready.

'I'm going around the table with the first question. Did you leave your table this evening?' Harry pointed to a man on his left. 'You sir.'

'No.'

The same reply came from everyone until Harry got to Fred Anstey. He grumbled saying they already knew about him going looking for Natasha.

Apart from Mr Anstey, Natasha Poole was the only person who'd left the room. Harry asked if anyone had seen anyone moving about or going down the corridor. No one had.

Harry and Bradley left Sara and Charlotte in charge and went out to the Oak Room.

18

Harry and Bradley walked towards the fireplace.

'Here,' said the man sitting at the small table for two, 'we've been waiting a long time for our bill. It's not right keeping us here against our will.'

'Sorry about that sir,' said Bradley.

Harry looked around for Lucy. She and Donna were at the end of the room. This man hadn't yet heard that he wouldn't be charged.

'Would you answer a few questions, please?' asked Bradley. 'All being well, we will start allowing people to leave soon.'

'I should think so too!'

When asked, the couple said they hadn't noticed anything as their table was a bit removed from most of the others. The man complained that service had been slow but admitted, resentfully, that he supposed there had been a reason for that.

Harry and Bradley moved to the table for four by the window, the one next to Johnny Rouse and Rochelle.

People's answers were distressingly similar. No one had

seen or heard anything. No one had moved since they had sat down. It was such a shame someone was hurt. Where was the ambulance? Wasn't it so kind of Lucy not to charge them? They'd really like to pay. After thanking the diners, Harry moved past Rochelle, who was busy texting, to the table beyond her, a small round table for two.

An elderly couple were seated there. The man held a cane. His hand shook. His companion, probably his wife, was a few years younger than him.

Harry asked if they had left their table during the evening. They both said they hadn't. He was on the point of asking if they'd noticed anyone else leave their table when the woman inclined her head towards Rochelle.

'She,' whispered the woman, 'and her man were all lovey dovey one minute and arguing the next. He was fiddling with his phone all evening. Just like my grandson. So inappropriate at the dinner table. But they all do it you know.'

Harry nodded slowly, as though he was agreeing. He didn't. Mobile phones were just a fact of life now.

'Did you notice anyone leaving their table?'

'He got up and left.'

'He?'

'The man with that young woman.'

'You saw him get up?'

'I did. He just got up and left. Left her alone. I felt a bit sorry for her but now she's complaining, which is annoying, and where has her young man gone?'

'Thank you,' said Harry, making a note.

Lucy and Donna were now at the table with Rochelle. The young woman was weeping and asking where Johnny Rouse was. Harry could hear Donna trying to calm her.

A knock came to the front door, following by a loud rap on the nearby window. A young woman, who seemed heavily pregnant, was tapping the window and looking at Rochelle. She was mouthing something, but Harry couldn't hear.

Rochelle jumped up. 'That's her! That's his wife! Oh I have to hide!'

'Sit down, Rochelle,' said Harry.

Rochelle sat, then jumped up again. 'But, but, her… '

'Sit down and stay down. Turn your back to the window. Okay?'

A loud sniff was all the answer he got, but Rochelle sat and did as he asked.

The room was suddenly quiet. Everyone was listening and watching.

Harry inclined his head at Bradley. They moved to the corridor and stepped behind the screen.

'The woman outside,' said Harry. 'She looks like she's expecting so I'm thinking she must be Johnny Rouse's wife. Here,' he gave Bradley the set of keys Donna had produced. 'Will you go out and talk to her?'

* * * * *

Returning to the Oak Room, Harry walked down to a long bench at the end wall. Two tables were drawn up to it. One by the window, for six, and a smaller table for four near to the kitchen door.

A young man at the window end of the table, who had been sitting slumped, sat up straight. This was the man whom Sara had seen going down the corridor. He and the young woman seated opposite him. She was wearing a wedding ring so most likely man and wife. The other occupants of the table were much older.

The young man looked stressed now. His eyes were darting from Harry, to the window, then back to Harry.

Just as Harry was about to speak, an older man addressed the young man.

'You left the table, didn't you mate?'

'Me, yeah. Went for a sl– went to the toilet.'

The young woman drew a deep breath in noisily through her nose. She opened her mouth as though to speak, but her table companion carried on talking.

'And you went too, didn't you Kylie?'

'Yeah. Had to. But I was only gone a minute like.'

Harry made notes but decided against saying anything for now. This was confirmation of what he's been told by Sara and Tom Black. He needed interview spaces, quickly. The people at this table should be separated. He didn't want them cooking up a story together.

Bradley came back. He locked the front door behind him, and beckoned to Harry. As they headed down the corridor again, Harry thought wryly that all the exercise they were getting should be good for them. Work off some of the Beef Wellington. Shame he hadn't finished it.

'The woman outside says she's Mrs Rouse and she's looking for her husband. She wants to know why the front door is locked.'

'What did you say?'

'I told her we had trouble from hooligans earlier and we locked it to keep them out. She said she'd spoken to her husband on the phone and she knew he was here because she has an app on his phone to let her know where he is. I asked her to go home. I said her husband would follow soon.'

'And did she?'

'I don't think so. She moved up the road and started dialling on her phone. Probably calling her husband.'

'Right. I think he said his phone was on mute, but answering will be impossible given that he's handcuffed.

However, that confirms parts of Johnny Rouse's story. Bradley, I want to separate the people at the end table by the window.'

'How are we to do that?'

'Perhaps take a couple of them to the Function Room? But we will have to wait a while. I don't want to raise their suspicions.'

'Why are you suspicious of them?'

'Because one of them said that the younger man by the window and the woman opposite him, left the table during their meal.'

'Can we corroborate that with what Sara saw?'

'Yes. So we're closing in. Bradley, would you phone Cambridge and ask them to check what's holding up the Ely squad car? If we could put a PC standing by that table, it would shut down any conversation between the six of them.'

'Will do, Harry.'

'After that, would you go to the tables close to the kitchen door? I'll go back to the window table. Seeing two of us close by might deter conversation. We'll compare notes afterwards, before moving on to Tom Black's group.'

As they pushed through the screen, Harry saw Sara pause at the end of the corridor.

'Where to next?' she asked.

'Start at the fireplace and work down the room on the window side, please Sara.'

Harry returned to the group of six. 'Give me your names, please.'

'Why?' asked a large woman. 'We didn't do anything. It was those two, the Leonards.'

Harry leaned in close to the woman. 'I'm taking everyone's name. Do you understand?'

The woman shivered, but Harry thought it was more from anger than fear.

'Ida Manners, Mrs. And this is–'

'I'd like everyone to speak for themselves.'

'Walter Manners.'

'Mick Gotobed.'

'Jane Gotobed.'

'Paul Leonard.'

'Kylie Leonard. Why are we being treated like criminals?'

''Taking names at the scene of an accident is standard procedure, Mrs Leonard.' Harry looked at each of the diners independently. 'I would like you to stay quiet until I can arrange a space to have a fuller conversation. Do you understand?'

They all nodded. Harry hoped they were sufficiently intimidated to halt any talking.

Harry noticed Lucy and Donna heading towards the corridor. He followed them. He ought to speak to the waitresses. Tom Black could wait a while. Harry already knew he'd left his table so there shouldn't be any surprises in what they might say.

He'd only turned the corner when a shout sounded from the restaurant.

19

It was Paul Leonard. He was trying to get out through the fire exit which was close to his table. Walter Manners and Mick Gotobed were holding him back.

There was mild mayhem in the Oak Room. People were standing by their tables, mostly. Voices were rising in distress and panic.

'Let me go. Let me go!'

Harry and Bradley each took an arm and hauled the man across the room and over to the bottom of the stairs.

'Let me go!' he shouted again.

Agnes barged through the inner kitchen door. 'You leave that man alone.'

'Get back to the kitchen, Agnes.'

Agnes started to go down past the tables. Heading for the corridor, Harry thought. 'Go through the restaurant, please.'

Agnes hesitated, looking from Harry to Mr Leonard.

'Go,' said Harry, firmly, wishing that help would arrive in the next few seconds because they were getting closer and closer to the tipping point with the diners.

Agnes has lowered her head. She looked like a bull about to charge. The spectacle of Agnes and her cousin, who was thrashing about, quietened everyone down. You could hear a pin drop in the room as people waited to see what would happen next.

Donna appeared, as though by magic. She laid her hands on Agnes's shoulders, turned her around, and marched her into the kitchen through the door at the end of the Oak Room.

The sigh of relief was almost audible. Donna was a safe pair of hands. Harry thought he would have to put her forward for a commendation or a medal or something. She was managing where he and Bradley were struggling.

As if to reinforce that thought, Paul Leonard tried to pull away.

'Calm down!' said Harry. He and Bradley half-dragged the man towards the corridor. 'We're going to the far side of this screen, and then you can tell us why you were trying to get away.'

Bradley opened the panel in the screen and Harry pushed Paul Leonard through as soon as the opening was wide enough. He pushed it back into place, turned and looked at Mr Leonard. There was no need to put on a strict face. Harry was furious.

'I've just had enough, haven't I?' said Mr Leonard. 'This was supposed to be a fun night. It's turning into a funeral.' He suddenly stopped talking. Despite the low light, Harry saw the man's face was ashen. Did he know that Natasha Poole was dead?

'Everyone is having to deal with what has happened, sir. If you stand still and answer my questions, we will let go of your arms.'

The man stopped resisting. Harry and Bradley let go but Harry saw that Bradley was ready to make another grab if he needed to. The man shook himself, cracked his neck. Stood still.

'Now,' said Harry, 'may I have your name?'

'I've already told you. It's Paul, Paul Leonard.'

'Leonard? Any relation to Agnes?'

'Yeah. We're cousins.'

Bradley nodded at Harry. 'I'll double-check.'

'Do you live in Soham, Mr Leonard?'

'Yeah.'

'We need an explanation for your sudden bid to leave the restaurant.'

'I don't want to go to the copshop.'

'You may have no choice. We'll take your statement here, firstly. If it checks out, you'll be free to leave. Until then, you must stay on the premises.'

Paul Leonard backed away from Harry.

'It wasn't me. I never hurt her. I wouldn't do that. I never caused an accident.'

'Her?' asked Harry.

The man kept backing away. Before Harry could grab him, he'd backed through the curtain into the bar. Harry pushed in after him. Mr Leonard seemed to realise where he was. He turned around.

Harry watched Paul Leonard's reaction as he noticed the dead woman on the sofa.

'Natasha,' he called to her. 'Natasha?' His jaw had fallen open. He moved towards the body as Harry went to grab him. 'What's wrong, darling? What's wrong? You don't look well, you're pale.'

Harry put a hand on Paul Leonard's arm to stop the man moving closer to the body. 'She's dead. Mr Leonard. Natasha Poole is dead.'

Once again, utter silence descended.

Paul Leonard fell to the floor in a dead faint. Harry

caught him before he hit his head off the coffee table. He laid the man on the floor, trying to take most of the weight on his good arm.

He dialled Bradley's mobile. 'Hey Harry,' said Bradley. 'Agnes is indeed Paul Leonard's cousin.'

'Come to the bar immediately.'

They checked the unconscious man together. Bradley took a pin from the back of his jacket lapel and stuck it into the man's hand. Paul Leonard didn't move. He really had passed out.

'He knew Natasha Poole,' said Harry.

'But it seems he didn't know she was dead.'

'It does seem so.'

Just then, Harry heard the welcome sound of a police car siren.

'At last! Take over Bradley. Sit on the man if you have to. Let me have the keys.'

* * * * *

Harry ran back to the Oak Room. The police car was outside with its lights flashing. Two PCs were waiting at the door.

'Turn off the lights,' Harry said as he opened up. 'Drive the car around the corner, to the car park at the back. It'll be less obvious there.'

One officer sat into the car, turned off the flashing blue lights, and drove away. Harry led the other PC down to the bar.

'Whoa, what have we got here?'

'A dead body and a suspect,' replied Harry. 'What took you so long to get here? Ely's only a few miles away.'

'We would have been here sooner but a tractor overturned by the Barway turnoff. A sudden gust, the driver said. Storm Darragh hasn't finished with us yet. A load of celery fell all over the road. We had to pick the stuff up by hand. There was a lot of celery on that trailer. Then we had to stay with the accident until another squad car came out to take over directing the traffic.'

'Right. Do you have a set of cuffs?'

'Of course!' The PC picked a pair from the back of his uniform.

'Great. Cuff this man, then help us to get him into that building at the back of the patio.' Harry waved in the direction of the Function Room.

'We phoned through to explain the delay,' said the policeman, 'but no one had the name of the officer who asked us to come out so we couldn't send you a message.'

'Don't worry about it. What's your name?'

'I'm Pete Saunders. My colleague is Dev Patel. That'll be him,' said Pete as PC Patel knocked on the fire escape door.

'I'm DI Harry Meredith, this is DS Bradley West.'

They rolled Paul Leonard over, cuffed him, and carried him across the garden into the Function Room. Harry let Bradley and the PCs take most of the weight. His bad arm was getting too much work this evening.

'Pete, will you go back to the main restaurant, please. Stand by the front door. I'll be with you shortly. Dev, will you stay here with Mr Leonard? Bradley, you were in the kitchen. Do you need to go back?'

'Yes, I'd just begun to question Agnes.'

20

Bradley had asked everyone aside from Agnes Leonard to leave the kitchen while he answered Harry's call, but Vi was still there when he returned.

'Will you go into the Oak Room please?' he asked.

'Why? Why does she have to go?' asked Agnes.

'I want to speak to you alone, for the moment.'

Vi went through the door into the restaurant. Bradley wondered if that was a good decision. Agnes was trouble. What if she forced a difficult situation? He really should have a third person present. It was too late to remedy that now. He focussed on Agnes.

'So you know Paul Leonard?'

'Yeah. He's a cousin. He's in the restaurant this evening with his wife.'

'Did you speak to him this evening?'

'No.' Agnes batted her eyes a few times. Bradley was sure she was lying. 'I've been waiting on the group in the Victorian Room. Paul and I nodded hello, but that's it. His family and mine aren't very close. He's, like a second cousin or something.'

'So you didn't speak to him this evening?'

'Well I might have nodded to him, but we didn't talk.'

Her eyes were going again and a flush was creeping up her neck.

'How did you know he was in the restaurant?'

'Well he told me he was coming, didn't he? And I saw him earlier outside in the corridor. He was probably going to the toilet.'

Good, thought Bradley. We now have a witness putting a suspect near the scene. He scribbled in his notebook.

'And you didn't talk to each other?'

'I might have said 'Hi'.'

'How did he seem? Did he say 'Hi' back?'

'He hardly said anything. He, like, almost pushed past me which could have been awkward 'cos I was carrying a load of empty plates.'

So Agnes could get angry with her relatives as well as the police. Nice to know she was grumpy all round.

'Did you see him go to the toilet?'

'Ugh no. I'm not a pervert.'

Bradley supposed he'd asked for that response, given the clumsy way he'd asked the question.

'I went into the kitchen. I had a full tray-load of dirty plates! So why do you want to know all this?"

Bradley was surprised Agnes hadn't challenged him earlier in the conversation. She certainly was a feisty character. Right now, she was standing in the kitchen, arms akimbo, eyebrows raised.

So far as Bradley knew, Agnes had done nothing wrong. Families were often difficult to question. They frequently banded together to protect their own and keep the police out.

Bradley decided to stop questioning Agnes. She was a slippery customer and he would get nowhere. Sitting her down and speaking to her formally was the best option. It might help her understand how serious the matter was. Might. She would have to be called as a witness now they knew she had seen Paul Leonard in the corridor, but her relationship to the suspect had turned her into a semi-hostile witness.

Bradley heard a thumping sound from the corridor. He needed to end the conversation and get back to Harry.

'Don't read too much into this, Agnes,' he said. 'We're questioning a lot of people. Paul Leonard has already told us he went to the toilet earlier in the evening. We're simply trying to build up a picture of what happened. Thank you for being helpful.'

Bradley went to the door leading to the corridor. Agnes followed him. He stopped in front of the door. 'You should use the other entrance, Agnes. We want to keep this corridor free now.'

'Why?'

'Please use the other door.'

Bradley waited until Agnes backed into the kitchen, then slipped into the corridor. It was empty. He stood a moment by the curtain to the bar.

A creaking sound made him turn back. There was Agnes, peering out at him. He walked up to the door and stared at her. It was the only method of persuasion he had. She wasn't the only one with a stare that would open an oyster at sixty paces, he thought, calling up a phrase from P G Woodhouse. It often helped him laugh and come back to a normal place. But he didn't feel like laughing now. He, Harry and Oog were in a small place, a woman had been murdered, and he actually felt like they were trying to find the killer in a can of sardines.

The kitchen door closed. Bradley gave it a slight push. It held steady. He didn't think Agnes would open it again, but he couldn't stop her. Slipping back to the curtain, he cracked it open. Harry had returned.

'Wasn't Leonard one of the people Sara saw leaving their table?' asked Bradley.

'Yes. If only we could establish timings?'

A noise from the corridor silenced them. It sounded like someone was trying the doors to the toilets. Thank goodness Bradley and Oog had locked them.

'Hello?' came a voice.

Harry slid back through the curtain.

21

Kylie Leonard was opening the door to the kitchen.

'Hello,' he called, crossing to the door. 'What are you doing here?'

How did she get down the corridor without being stopped? What was PC Pete doing?

The woman let her hand drop from the door handle. 'I'm looking for my husband. The toilets are locked and I can't see him. Where have you put him?'

'The man who tried to get out through the fire exit? He's your husband?'

'He is. What have you done with him? He hasn't done anything wrong. He's been with me all evening.'

'Mrs Leonard?'

'I told you I was Paul's wife. Can't you let him go? We should be leaving. We have a babysitter and she needs to go home.'

'Your husband is helping us at the moment, Mrs Leonard. It won't be possible for him to leave. Anything you can tell me about the evening would be helpful, however.'

'I've told you he's done nothing. He was worried about the babysitter, as am I. He simply wanted to get out and go home. Do you have children, Inspector? Do you understand the worry they cause? You have to free him.'

'Did Mr Leonard leave the table during the evening?'

'He might have gone to the toilet but he came straight back. He was only gone half a minute.'

'Did you leave the table, Mrs Leonard?'

'No.'

'Okay. I'd like you to return to your table for the present please, and I want you to stay there. We will be taking a statement from you in a little while.'

Kylie Leonard whipped around and tramped down the corridor. Harry had to move fast to keep up with her. She stopped suddenly as she turned into the Oak Room. Harry almost bumped into her. He looked quickly down to where she'd been sitting. The table was empty. Where–Ah. The four people who'd been sitting with her previously had moved away. They were talking to Sara at Harry's table.

Mrs Leonard carried on walking down the room. She slowed a bit as she passed, stared at the large woman, who immediately went red, then carried on.

Vi was standing by the door to the kitchen. It opened out, pushing her forwards. Agnes came into the room. She went straight to Mrs Leonard's table. Harry moved swiftly towards her.

'Agnes, Vi, can you return to the kitchen, please?'

'But I only wanted to talk to my cousin!' said Agnes.

'You can do that later. Please return to the kitchen for now.'

Vi hurried into the kitchen. Agnes stood stubbornly in front of Harry, who stood just as firmly in front of her. He would later be amused when Bradley recounted his impression of Agnes's stare. Harry had been a policeman for many years, however, and he had out-stared many troublesome people in his time. Agnes finally gave way and backed into the kitchen. If it hadn't been a swing door, Harry was sure it would have been shut with a healthy slam.

What would the pestilent girl do next?

He turned back to Kylie Leonard. 'Stay at this table, Mrs Leonard, until I come back for you. Do you understand?'

Her eyes were flaming, but she nodded her assent.

* * * * *

As he was returning to the bar, Harry found Donna and Lucy in the corridor outside the door to the kitchen.

Donna signalled him to stop. She placed a finger over her lips. 'Agnes,' she whispered, 'says you've arrested her cousin for the murder. She's very angry. You can hear her complaining to the others.'

Harry didn't need to put his head close to the door. He could hear Agnes loudly and clearly. 'A lot is happening all at once,' he said. 'We haven't arrested Agnes's cousin, but he will be helping us with our enquiries.'

'Where is he?'

'In the Function Room. He pushed his way into the bar.'

'Into the bar?' said Lucy, raising her voice.

Donna grabbed her arm. 'Shussh.'

'Sorry,' whispered Lucy. 'Did he see the body?'

'He got into the bar before we could stop him and saw Natasha Poole. He fainted. It's clear that he knew her. He's out cold and under guard in the Function Room.'

Harry glanced at his watch. It had been almost half an hour since Bradley had phoned through to the Incident Room in Cambridge. The team should soon arrive. He wondered, briefly, if they too were being delayed by the overturned tractor. But he realised they would come along the A14 and approach Soham from a different direction. So they should arrive quite soon.

'I think we can start letting those we're certain didn't come down the corridor go home now. But not Fred Anstey from Geoff Norman's group, and not Geoff himself as he's a witness. I'll be asking the people who were sitting next to Natasha Poole to stay also.'

'Okay Harry,' said Donna. 'I'll note them on the floorplan. I'll go back to the front door to check people as they leave. Okay?'

'It would also be good if we could empty the carpark,' said Harry. 'The Incident Van and police vehicles will park there, and we ought to seal the place from the back.'

'Would you ask them not to use the flashing blue lights, please Harry?' asked Lucy. 'It attracts too much attention. My heart almost stopped when I saw the squad car earlier.'

'We'll ask them to turn them off, but they may be on when they arrive.'

Lucy and Donna looked sombre. Harry felt sorry for them. He would ask Bradley to phone through to the van and cars.

Harry squeezed back into the bar. Bradley was waiting for him.

'Did you hear that exchange, Bradley? Will you contact the Incident Van and cars and ask them not to use the sirens or lights? Lucy would appreciate us keeping things as low key as possible. I'm going down to the Oak Room. I need to find out why the PC let Mrs Leonard come down the corridor.'

'Yeah, that was odd.'

'Then I'll go to the Victorian Room. I will ask everyone who was not involved with Natasha Poole to get ready to leave. When you're free, will you join me and stay with the remainder? Process them in batches of four so as not to build up a long queue in the Oak Room.

'Quick catch-up, Harry. Agnes saw her cousin in the corridor earlier.'

'Another witness. She may know more. I think we'll save questioning her until we've reduced the number of people in the restaurant. She's a tricky customer.'

'You're not wrong. Okay, I'll go over the Oak Room names with Donna so we can clear out that room too.'

Harry went into the kitchen on his way past. Donna was there, keeping the peace, he thought, if the look on Agnes's face was anything to go by.

'We'll need the staff to stay so we can get statements from them.'

'All three?'

'Yes. They may have seen things as they trekked to and fro with meals and drinks and that. If you could come back to the Oak Room with me, we'll start clearing people so they can leave.'

'Sure Harry. Just one problem.'

'What's that, Donna?'

'Elsie has run off.'

22

Sara's table had been commandeered by four of the people who had been sitting with Mr and Mrs Leonard. They were refusing to go back to their own table.

Ida Manners introduced herself. 'Paul Leonard lied. We don't want to be associated with a killer.'

'He may be perfectly innocent,' replied Sara, adding as she remembered what Harry had said, 'and we've only been told about an accident.'

'Whatever. He's a selfish man and his wife has a proper temper on her. She's been trying to butter me up. I'm a district councillor, you know. I'm important. She wants to get a change of use on a café so she can open a hairdresser. Using me. It's not acceptable. And her married to a killer! I, I… Think of the damage that could do to my reputation? No, we're staying put here, thank you very much.'

Under cover of the table, Sara touched her shoe to Charlotte's to get her attention. Charlotte wrinkled her forehead before widening her eyes in understanding. 'I need a glass of water,' she said.

'There's water here on the table,' said Mrs Manners.

'Aren't you feeling well, Charlotte?' asked Sara. They needed to get away. 'Come and stand by the coats. I'll see if we can open a window for air.'

'Oh lovely!' Mrs Manners sniffed. 'Nice to have friends in high places.'

Sara looked back a moment as she and Charlotte abandoned their table. A memory or an impression, had floated up from somewhere, but she couldn't catch it. Perhaps it wasn't important. Maybe it was nothing to do with the murder. She let it go as she spotted Harry and Donna slipping through the screen. She and Charlotte moved towards the coat hooks.

Harry joined them. 'Good, you're alone. I want to speak to you both. I'll be back shortly. Donna, will you stay by the front door, please? I want to have a word with PC Pete.'

Harry signalled to the PC to follow him down the corridor. Sara wondered what had happened. Things were going a bit crazy. It must be so difficult to corral a large group of people some of whom would not want to play along. It certainly hadn't worked with Mr Rouse or Mr Leonard. Who would be the next person to kick out at the restraint?

Harry came back with the PC, whose neck and face were flushed.

'So what did you say to him, Harry?' asked Sara.

'I left him in charge here and yet Mrs Leonard managed to sneak down the corridor. He said he turned his back for a moment to answer a question from the couple by the fireplace. When you're on guard, you're on guard. You don't turn your back to anything. He won't do that again.'

Oh dear. Harry could be really tough when he put his mind to it. The poor PC.

'Now, back to business. We need to start letting people go. We'll begin with the Victorian Room. Sara, do you have the lists of names and addresses?'

'I do. Sara patted her bag.

'I'd like you to check people off as they line up to leave. Charlotte, will you then usher the people to the front door? Do it in batches of four. Donna will double check them against her list, and let them out.'

* * * * *

Harry stood once again in the Victorian Room. 'Everyone, may I have your attention. Could anyone who was sitting beside Natasha Poole this evening, or who had significant conversation with her, come together in a group at the end of the room. Geoff, would you and Fred Anstey join that group, please?'

People stood up and began shuffling. Four women made their way to the end of the room.

'Thank you. Those not in that group, please form a queue by my colleagues Sara and Charlotte. It's time for you to leave the restaurant. Sara will check you off the lists and Charlotte will walk you to the front door where Donna is waiting. Please leave promptly. I understand the temptation will be to gather in the carpark, but I would ask you to move your vehicle and drive off as quickly as you can. We have an ambulance and squad car coming out from Cambridge and they will need the space.'

'Why didn't the ambulance come from Ely?' asked one of the women who'd spoken with Natasha.

'A tractor has overturned on the A142 Soham to Ely road. It lost its load and is being cleared up. The ambulance is already on the way from Cambridge.'

Harry went to speak to the group gathered at the end

of the room. The remainder, now surprisingly quiet, stood in a line by Sara. She processed people as Harry had requested before passing them to Charlotte who escorted the little groups to the front door.

Sara listened as Harry spoke to those who had been asked to stay behind.

'Could you please make notes of anything you observed this evening, or anything you think might be helpful. Please don't confer. Here are sheets to write statements on. We will go through them as soon as we can. You will then be free to leave.'

'Geoff,' said Harry, 'I'd like you to write up a statement, but will you stay behind when the others have left, please?'

'Sure.'

As he left the Victorian Room, Harry stopped close to Sara. 'We'll carry on talking to people in the Oak Room in the same manner. We'll go from table to table, starting with table 6 by the fire.'

'What will we do with anyone you want to hold back?'

'They'll have to stay at their table for now. I don't want unconnected people chatting together.'

Sara saw Harry glance at the group of four sitting at the table which had been theirs.

'They wanted to get away from the man who tried to leave through the fire escape,' she told him. 'They won't go back. The woman in the flowery dress, Mrs Manners, doesn't trust the guy's wife.'

'Ah. Right. Okay, Sara, let's thin down the numbers.'

23

Rochelle was watching people trooping out the door. 'Why can't I go too?' she whinged. 'It's not fair, picking on me. And where's Johnny? He should be let go too.'

'You'll be free to go once we collect and check statements. It won't be long.'

Rochelle muttered, shook her head but she did stay at her table.

Mrs Manners leaned across to Rochelle. 'Give it over. If you stay quiet we'll get out a lot sooner.'

'I won't stay quiet. I'm going to make a complaint.'

'You're welcome to make a complaint,' said Harry, who overheard the exchange. 'More police are due to arrive shortly. Once your statement and fingerprints have been taken, you can give your complaint to one of the officers. Until then, kindly sit down and stay quiet.'

It was probably the mention of fingerprints being taken, but Rochelle looked horrified. She shut up, took out her phone and began texting. Harry wondered how soon her phone would run out of battery. She was using it whenever he looked her way.

Mrs Leonard was now the sole occupant of table 10. She grabbed her bag and stood up as Harry approached.

'Sit down, Mrs Leonard. We'll come back to you.'

Her loud intake of breath made it obvious that the woman wasn't happy, but she had the sense to sit back down. Rochelle could take lessons from Mrs Leonard.

Between them, Harry, Sara and Charlotte soon dispatched the majority of the diners.

Harry crossed to Mrs Manners and her companions. 'Why have you moved?'

'We're not sitting with her!' She shook her head in Mrs Leonard's direction.

'Fine. You can all stay there until we're ready to talk to you.'

Harry went to the final table, Tom Black's. He'd been aware that Tom had been watching the proceedings carefully.

'I suppose you'll want a statement from me?' said Tom.

'Yes. We'll have to wait until the Victorian Room is free. Sorry for the delay.'

'Yeah, but my wife and friends are getting tired. It's time we all went home. I can tell you now that it will be an easy statement. I went down the corridor for a slash. But the others all stayed here. Didn't you?'

Mr and Mrs Sparks nodded their heads. They were like birds, timid frightened birds.

'Do we have your names and addresses, phone numbers?' Harry glanced at the people and raised his eyebrows at Sara.

The diners nodded.

'We do,' added Sara.

'Okay, you three can go,' he said to the Sparks and Mrs Black. 'We need Tom to stay as he's a witness. Did you drive here together?'

'No, Inspector,' said Tom. 'Me and the Mrs came in my car and David and Clarice came in David's car.' Before Harry could reply, Tom nodded to David. 'Give the Mrs a lift home, will you? I'll catch you later.'

'Oh Tommy!'

'Off you go, pigeon. David will drop you home.'

Nodding her head as if she really was one, 'Pigeon' stood her ground. 'I'll stay with you, Tommy.'

'You'll be better going home now, Pammy.'

But Pammy sat back down by her husband. At a nod from Tom, David and Clarice left. Sara marked them off her list.

A loud rap sounded on the front door. Donna jumped. She opened the door and two uniformed policemen came in.

'Where do you want us, Harry,' asked the lead policeman.

24

Harry heaved an inward sigh of relief as Terry and Carlos entered the restaurant. He knew both well.

'Let's go around to the car park.'

Harry sucked in the fresh air as they walked around the corner. The wind had all but died down. One squad car was parked a little way up the road on double yellows.

'That must belong to the Ely crew,' said Carlos as they turned into the car park. 'Our car is here.'

There was plenty of room for the Incident Van. Two officers were in the gowning tent, which had been set up against the side of the Van, donning forensic overalls.

Harry entered the tent and greeted Mariama, the senior forensic technician, and her assistant, Ted.

'Quick outline. A female has been stabbed. She's in the bar. We've been as careful as possible but there will be cross-contamination as the scene wasn't fully secured. One of the diners pushed into the room and passed out. He didn't touch the body. We're holding him in the Function Room.' Harry pointed to a building backing onto the car park. 'There is an entrance to the kitchen behind us. The door is unlocked for fire regulation reasons. I will return to the restaurant now and open the fire door in the bar to give you direct access.'

'How many customers are there?' asked Mariama.

'About fifty. We've let a lot go. Currently, we have five suspects. And two staff who must be cleared. All were in the corridor which leads to the murder scene at some point during the evening. They need to be finger-printed.'

Mariama nodded. 'We'll get that kit set up and collect prints from the bar to compare with. We'll let you know as soon as it's possible which of those from your group can be eliminated forensically That should narrow things down.'

'We have what we believe is the murder weapon.'

'You've been working hard, Harry. What is it?'

'A small knife. And I didn't find it. Oog did.'

'Oog? He's here?' Mariama looked surprised.

'We came here to Soham for dinner. A leaving dinner for Oog, actually. Ah, you need to fingerprint him because we won't have his prints on file, and also our two guests, Sara Engemann and Charlotte Brown.'

'I see. Well it's great you have the knife. We'll make a start on that, then Carlos can begin collecting fingerprints.'

'The knife was found in a toilet so the killer may have wiped it clean. Over to you on all of that. I'll head back and open the fire escape door. It surprises me that the killer didn't use it to escape, but perhaps they realised the alarm would go off. We don't think he or she left, though we can't be 100% sure about that.'

'Is there CCTV?'

'No. I checked with Lucy and Donna. The owners,' he added, when Mariama looked puzzled.

* * * * *

Soon, Harry was leading the white-clad team into the bar. He explained what had happened since discovering Natasha Poole's body.

'That's Bradley's SoC box. This,' Harry pointed to the lemon-cutting knife in an evidence bag, 'is what we believe was used to stab the victim.'

'Thanks Harry. We'll make a start.'

*****

Harry went back to the Oak Room. It was quiet there. The entry of more uniformed police probably brought the seriousness of the crime home to the diners who remained. They must have realised by now that it was far more serious than an accident.

PC Pete was standing by the entrance, with his back to the fireplace. The fire had almost died away, leaving a few glowing embers.

Harry nodded to Sara and Charlotte. He noticed the strain on Charlotte's face. What a way for a promising date to end. Would she stick with Bradley after this baptism of fire? He hoped so. She'd been such a help.

Sara also looked tired.

Looking at the faces of those remaining in the main restaurant room, Harry noted that Mrs Leonard was still impossible to read, and Rochelle was slumped over her table. The four people who had hijacked Harry's own table were sitting bolt upright, staring at him as though their life depended on knowing what he was up to. Tom Black nodded to Harry. He was sitting quietly beside his wife, unruffled and patient.

Bradley was in the Victorian Room with Oog.

'Terry relieved me. And he has given me back my handcuffs.' Oog was meticulously placing them back into their plastic container.

'You can stand down now, Oog. I am so grateful to you for your help.'

'*Pas de problème*. I was happy to help.'

'We can debrief later. I want to get statements from everyone and then we'll decide who to hang onto and who to let go. Why not join Sara and Charlotte?'

'*D'accord*, Harry.'

Oog went off. Harry hoped he would cheer up Sara and Charlotte. They needed to sit down, that pair. He and Bradley would try to clear the people out of this room, and then it could be used as an interview space. He didn't think it would take long to let Mrs Manner's gang of four go home, then that table would also be free.

Bradley waved the sheaf of papers he held. 'I have statements from the ex-Young Farmers. Two of them were sitting by victim, and two across the table from her. They all spoke to Natasha Poole. We need to question Mr Anstey more closely. Geoff Norman has played a part for much of the evening, so we will need to get a comprehensive statement from him too.'

'Thanks, Bradley.' Harry went and stood by the dresser to read the statements.'

25

WITNESS STATEMENT

Statement of: *Julie Bidwell*
Age if under 18: *over 18* Occupation: *Entrepreneur*

This statement (consisting of 1 page(s) each signed by me) is true to the best of my knowledge and belief and I make it knowing that, if it is tendered in evidence, I shall be liable to prosecution if I have wilfully stated in it anything which I know to be false, or do not believe to be true.
Witness Signature: *Julie Bidwell* Date: *07/12/2024*

I am the abovenamed. I came to the Red Lion for our annual Young Farmers Christmas dinner. I did not know Natasha Poole before this evening. She came with Fred Anstey and was sitting opposite me at the table. She seemed a lovely woman. We talked about her work. She said she was a teacher in Ely. I didn't ask where she met Fred as I didn't want to be nosey. We told her about how we knew each other in the Young Farmers group, which we have for over forty years. We met when we were young. Natasha was very surprised that we had kept in touch for such a long time. She knew nothing about farming. She said she had met Fred on a dating app. I didn't think they were well-matched.

I remember her saying "excuse me" before she left the table. I didn't realise she'd been gone so long until Geoff Norman was called out of the room by Donna.

We come to the Red Lion every year because the food is so good and we always have this big room which means we can sit around the table together. I hope the poor woman recovers from the accident.

---

* * * * *

WITNESS STATEMENT

Statement of: *Anne Chambers*

Age if under 18: *over 18* Occupation: *Retired*

This statement (consisting of 1 page(s) each signed by me) is true to the best of my knowledge and belief and I make it knowing that, if it is tendered in evidence, I shall be liable to prosecution if I have wilfully stated in it anything which I know to be false, or do not believe to be true.

Witness Signature: *A Chambers* Date: *07/12/2024*

I am the abovenamed person. I was sitting two away from Natasha Poole whom I only met this evening. What a nice woman. She came with Fred Anstey but he sat at the end of the table so I don't know how well they got on. We had a lot in common. She teaches in Ely, which she said suits her very well because she looks after her elderly mother and although she can't get to her during school hours, she has the long holidays when she can take her mum out for nice treats. She also does batch cooking then so her mum's freezer is loaded. What a kind caring person she is. I do hope the accident doesn't affect her mother's care as Natasha is an only child and the father died a few years ago.

As we were chatting, she said she and Fred met on a dating app. We were all interested to know how that works. Not that I'm going to use something like that, I work and have a happy busy life with family and friends, but we were all talking about it together.

I didn't see her leave the table. I must have turned away to talk to one of my friends. I wasn't really aware that she was gone until Geoffrey Norman went away. I noticed that because our dinner plates hadn't been removed and I looked around for him. Then the policeman told us there'd been an accident and we realised it must have happened to Natasha. Poor woman. I hope she gets well soon especially as Christmas is nearly here.

---

* * * * *

WITNESS STATEMENT

Statement of: *Sue Graham*

Age if under 18: *over 18* Occupation: *Entrepreneur*

This statement (consisting of 1 page(s) each signed by me) is true to the best of my knowledge and belief and I make it knowing that, if it is tendered in evidence, I shall be liable to prosecution if I have wilfully stated in it anything which I know to be false, or do not believe to be true.

Witness Signature: *Sue Graham* Date: *07/12/2024*

I am the abovenamed person.

I sat across the table from Natasha Poole. I was aware of a conversation about dating but I wasn't interested so I paid little heed and just talked to my neighbours at the table. This is the only time we get to catch up each year and I like seeing my old friends.

I didn't notice Natasha leaving the table. I didn't notice anything was wrong until the policeman told us there had been an accident. I do hope the woman hasn't been badly hurt.

* * * * *

WITNESS STATEMENT

Statement of: *Linda Parish*
Age if under 18: *over 18* Occupation: *Farmer*

This statement (consisting of 1 page(s) each signed by me) is true to the best of my knowledge and belief and I make it knowing that, if it is tendered in evidence, I shall be liable to prosecution if I have wilfully stated in it anything which I know to be false, or do not believe to be true.
Witness Signature: *Linda Parish* Date: *07/12/2024*

I am the abovenamed. I was sitting beside Natasha Poole at dinner. I have been coming to these annual dinners with my husband for many years. Geoffrey Norman has been organising them since Julie got so busy.

I hadn't met Natasha before this evening. She said she and Fred Anstey connected via a dating app. He paid her no attention the whole evening, because he was sitting at the end of the table with his friends. That was so rude. Poor woman. But she chatted away to us. She was intelligent. I don't know what she was doing with Fred.

I did notice that she had gone to the bathroom because she politely excused herself. I feel badly that I didn't do anything when she didn't come back. To be honest, I wondered if she'd simply gone home. I would if it had been me. It's not easy to be social with a big group of people you haven't met before especially when many of them are farmers. And the fact that Fred was ignoring her completely won't have helped. She did keep smiling but maybe she got tired of that. It can't have been easy for her.

I hope she soon gets better and that she stops going out with Fred who is a waste of space.

It was only us women who talked to her during dinner.

26

The arrival of extra uniformed police made Sara feel the evening had become even more sombre. Up to this point, it had been Harry and Bradley, with the help of Oog, who were conducting the investigation. She knew them all, and perhaps that had softened the sharp edge of the crime. Any softness there might have been had now vanished.

PC Pete was standing by the fireplace, stiff as a board, and watching everyone carefully. He reminded her of a Beefeater, the Irish Guards on sentry duty at Buckingham Palace. They always look unapproachable, seemingly blind to the public wandering before them, but clearly taking everything in. Sara had once looked up why they were called Beefeaters and discovered that they had been given a ration of beef each day. Protein to keep them alert and in good shape, she thought. The term reminded her of her meal of Beef Wellington. She hadn't finished it. In fact, she could see the plate still on her original table. Mrs Manners, who was sitting in Sara's former seat, had pushed all the plates into the middle of the table.

She, Charlotte and Oog had moved to the vacant table

for four close to the front door. Harry had taken their spot by the dresser. He had several pieces of paper in his hand. Sara watched him read each page, before returning to the Victorian Room.

Very soon, a group of four women emerged, followed by Harry. 'They're free to leave,' he said to Donna.

Four more down. Eight people remained in the Oak Room.

Donna disappeared briefly into the Victorian Room, then came back and fiddled with papers on the dresser.

Mrs Manners jumped up and went over to her. 'What is going on, Donna? When are we going to be let go? I don't like being here with the wife of a killer. It's upsetting.'

'Sorry my lovely, I'm sure the police will let you go very soon.'

'But do you know what's going on?'

'I know very little.' Donna lowered her voice but Sara could still hear what she said. 'It's not wise to say the woman on her own is the wife of a killer, Mrs Manners. What makes you think someone has been killed?'

'Because there are so many police here. I'm not stupid. That detective might be able to pull the wool over other people's eyes but I'm a district councillor. I see and hear about all sorts of dreadful behaviour in that role. And where is Paul Leonard if he hasn't been arrested? I ought to know! We ought to know. It's so upsetting that we have been sitting at a table all evening with a killer.' The woman began to sob.

'Go back to the table, Mrs Manners. I will ask the police to speak to you as soon as they can and then you'll be able to leave.'

'Thank you, Donna.' Mrs Manners sniffed and returned to the table to cry into a large white handkerchief she had withdrawn from a pocket.

Her companions at the table drew closer to her. There was much head-nodding going on.

Sara wasn't surprised at the change from the blustery woman who'd evicted them from their table earlier. The strain was getting to them all.

'When do you think they'll let us go?' asked Charlotte. 'How will we get home if Bradley isn't free? Do you think they'll finish up soon?'

'*Ma chère* Charlotte,' said Oog, reaching over and patting her hand. 'It is difficult, I know, but we must wait. I am certain that Harry and Bradley will organise a way for us to get back to Cambridge.'

'We could get a taxi,' said Sara, 'if that's the only option. I'd much prefer if we could travel together. I'd feel nervous in a taxi on my own. It's shocking being around a crime. It's the first time that has happened to me.'

'And yet, Sara, you have been close to Harry for many years, *n'est c'est pas*?'

'I have, but only on the periphery of crimes.'

Oog leaned close to Sara. "That couple, with the loud woman who was very nasty about the man's wife? They are staring at us. Perhaps we should stay quiet?'

'Why?' asked Charlotte. 'She's been nasty about other people, particularly that woman who's sitting alone. She's been maligning her. I don't care if she hears me say that.'

Oog rolled his eyes, shook his head and shut up.

Another person came out of the Victorian Room. It was Geoff Norman. Donna walked with him to the door. Bradley followed and let them out. Donna stood talking to Mr Norman before returning. So he'd been let go. They must be tightening in on the killer.

Bradley joined them and pulled up a chair close to Charlotte. 'Sorry about all this,' he put his arm around her shoulders.

'When can we leave, Bradley?' she asked.

'Quite soon, I think. We'll need statements from the three of you, but as you've been helping and close by us most of the evening, we've agreed that you can come to the station in the morning and give your statements there. We will need to take your fingerprints before you go, however.'

Charlotte looked as if she would cry.

'I appreciate that,' said Sara. 'We're quite tired now.'

'I know. Let me speak to Harry. Give us ten minutes.'

Bradley nodded to Oog and went back into the Victorian Room. Donna resumed her spot by the dresser.

Mrs Leonard, the woman sitting alone at the end table, stood up. She marched down the room and stopped by Donna. 'I want to leave, Donna. I see lots of people being let go. Can't you vouch for me? You know me. And after all, Agnes is a cousin.'

'It's not up to me, Kylie, but I think they're just taking statements and you should be able to give one soon.'

'Can you get the car key from Paul? Where is he by the way?'

'I don't know where he is. I'll ask about the key.'

'You'll ask?'

'It's all I can do. Sorry.'

Kylie Leonard tramped back to her table.

One of the Cambridge policemen followed her. He had an ink pad and a set of cards with him. He spoke softly but Mrs Leonard bristled. Sara understood. It wasn't a nice prospect. She supposed the PC would soon come to take their prints.

27

WITNESS STATEMENT

Statement of: *Geoffrey Norman*
Age if under 18: *over 18* Occupation: *Farmer*

This statement (consisting of 2 page(s) each signed by me) is true to the best of my knowledge and belief and I make it knowing that, if it is tendered in evidence, I shall be liable to prosecution if I have wilfully stated in it anything which I know to be false, or do not believe to be true.
Witness Signature: *G Norman* Date: *07/12/2024*

I am the abovenamed person. I was at the Red Lion for our annual Ex-Young Farmers Christmas dinner, which I book every year. I have been coming to the Red Lion for years.

I only met Natasha Poole this evening. I said hello to her when Fred Anstey introduced us. She seemed nice. I didn't notice her leaving the table but then I sitting at the other end so that's not surprising. The first I knew anything was wrong was when Donna asked me to help her with something. I followed her down the corridor to the bar. She introduced me to the Inspector, Harry Meredith. He took me into the bar and asked me if I knew Natasha. It was an awful shock to see her dead. I confirmed that it was Natasha though the inspector already knew her name. I was asked not to go back to our group, but to stand by the front door which Donna said she had locked, and to prevent people from leaving. I was a bit anxious about that because I'm not big and brawny. But Donna asked me to help and I agreed.

Later, my group were told to leave the Victorian Room. They gathered together at the top of the main dining room, it's called the Oak Room, and I joined them there. A man was taken into the Victorian Room. I don't know him. We heard him trying to escape through the French doors which lead to the garden. A lot of people were disturbed by that. He was moved out of the room afterwards and we were eventually allowed to return to our table. I was asked to keep an eye on the group. That was easy. They're all great people, not criminals, and no one tried to escape.

We talked about what had happened. I wasn't allowed to mention Natasha, but the others realised she was missing. Everyone wondered where she had gone. Fred Anstey got stroppy. I had to persuade him to stay quiet until the police came back.

Everyone was asking me what I knew and I had to tell them I wasn't allowed to say anything. So after that they began speculating and I hoped Harry would soon come and tell us something. Lucy and Donna came in with Harry. They said we would not be charged for our meals. That is very good of them and if they aren't charging anyone that must be costing them a lot of money.

Then Harry asked everyone if they'd left the room at any point but no one had except for Fred and they knew about that. Harry asked when we had last seen Natasha and then he left. We were alone for a long time before Harry came back again. He split us into two groups and asked the people who'd been sitting near Natasha to go to the end of the room. I was asked to join them. There were six of us. We were all asked to give statements. Julie, Annie, Linda and Sue were allowed to go soon after that, but I was asked to remain.

Fred Anstey and I were left in the Victorian Room. But as he's the one who brought Natasha to the dinner, that makes sense. It's such a shame that someone nice like Natasha was killed.

This is all I can think of. Any other questions, just ask.

---

* * * * *

WITNESS STATEMENT

Statement of: *Frederick Anstey*
Age if under 18: over 18 Occupation: *Retired*

This statement (consisting of 2 page(s) each signed by me) is true to the best of my knowledge and belief and I make it knowing that, if it is tendered in evidence, I shall be liable to prosecution if I have wilfully stated in it anything which I know to be false, or do not believe to be true.

Witness Signature: *Fred Anstey* Date: *07/12/2024*

I am Frederick Norbert Anstey. I was called Norbert after my grandfather on my mother's side.

I came to our annual Christmas Ex-Young Farmers party with a new girlfriend, Natasha Poole. I don't actually know her because we only met on Wednesday for half an hour. Of course I noticed she was missing. I think it was Annie who said she went to the toilet and didn't come back. I didn't pay any attention because I was with my friends and women always take a long time in the toilet so I waited for her to come back but she didn't and then I forgot about her. Besides, she's a grown woman.

After a while someone said they'd go and search for her but I couldn't have that because she was my girlfriend after all. I find women spend most of their time complaining about men being selfish and self-centred and mean and other difficult things. My ex-wife went on and on about that throughout most of the time we were married. I'm glad we didn't have kids because they might have taken after her and it would have driven me mad listening to more people in the house whinging.

So anyway, I got up and went down the corridor and the toilets doors were locked so I knocked and called her name. There was no answer so I knocked on the second door. But a man came out of the toilet instead. He was wearing plastic gloves which was very odd. I mean how does he wash them afterwards if he has gloves on? Then that arrogant police inspector, Merry or something, came along and he was very unpleasant.

He stopped me and started asking questions like what's my name and when did I last see Natasha. It had only been five minutes since I'd seen her, I swear. She was talking away with the other women so she was fine and I was with my friends and that was the whole point of the evening for me and I only brought her because last year some woman was asking when was I going to find a girlfriend as it had been two years since my divorce. Maybe a bit more now that I think of it. So I challenged Inspector Merry. He was sticking his nose into my personal business. He is still doing that. I should have been driven home long since. Instead I'm sitting in the dining room with Geoffrey. I'd like to know why. And how am I to get home when she's no longer able to drive? I'd like an answer to that too.

I did ask about Natasha so the inspector is a liar if he says I didn't. She'd only been gone five minutes when I went looking for her. She's a grown woman and I don't see why I should be responsible for her and if she's had an accident why can't she phone her family or a friend? I'm not taking responsibility for someone I don't even know. I was pushed out of the group and most of them have left by now and I'm innocent.

I went down the corridor only to look for Natasha. I haven't committed any crime. The only redeeming features about this evening are that I saw my friends and I'm not having to pay for my meal or the wine I drank.

I feel sorry for Natasha of course, but what happened to her isn't my fault.

28

Harry read Geoff Norman's and Fred Anstey's statements. 'What do you think, Bradley?'

'I think we could let Geoff Norman go, but we should hang onto Mr Anstey. Whatever did Natasha Poole see in the man?'

'There's never a definitive answer to what people see in each other. I agree though, we should hang onto Mr Anstey. Drunk as he was, he managed to get down the corridor. I want to hear about fingerprinting before we let him go.'

Harry pushed the dishes aside and spread out the statements on the table. 'So we have Leonard in the Function Room, Rouse upstairs in the office, and there are six other people to process, as well as Anstey. Let's leave Anstey in the Oak Room for now, Pete will keep him in order. Then bring the four who were together at the Leonard's table in here. We can spread them out and ask them to write statements. We need to get this table clear of clutter. I'll ask Donna to organise that.'

Donna, Agnes and Vi came in with trays and the table

was swiftly cleared. Harry had removed all the statements to keep them private and out of range of Agnes.

'Okay,' said Harry. 'Let's get Mr and Mrs Manners, and the Gotobeds in. Once we process them, we can speak to Mrs Leonard and then Tom Black. Oh.' Harry looked again at the table plan. 'We need to speak to Tom Black's wife too. She was sitting facing the corridor. I wonder what she saw?'

'I've told Charlotte and Sara that we'll take their statements tomorrow,' said Bradley. 'We know they're innocent.' He shook his head. 'I hate the way our world of crime has taken over our evening. What about Oog? Will there be a chance to have some sort of a jolly before he leaves?'

'I don't think so. He's heading back to Paris on Monday.'

"This evening has been a first.'

'Indeed, Bradley. Let's wind up. Sara and Charlotte can come to the station in Cambridge in the morning. We'll need their statements so we can get a full picture of what went on.'

'I should order a taxi to take them home.'

'I was thinking of asking Sara to drive back to Cambridge in my car – if she feels up to it.'

'It's annoying that I can't take Charlotte home. I hope she doesn't give up on me.'

'I doubt she will. She's been very helpful to us. Would she have been if she was irritated or fed up? Bradley, this is what your life is about. If you think this could become a serious relationship, then it's a difficult but good introduction for Charlotte.' Harry stopped a moment. 'Sorry. I hope that didn't come across as dismissive or insensitive? Being a copper stinks at times. The demands of the job have often overridden my personal concerns.

I'm sure that's true for you too.'

'It is, but it's a bummer when you're trying to start a new relationship.'

'Yeah.'

'Okay, Harry. I'll ask Pete to keep a beady eye on Anstey, and I'll bring the other four in. I'll spread them out along the table. That Mrs Manners is a forceful character.'

Harry gave a low laugh. 'I'll speak to the girls and Oog. I wonder if Carlos has fingerprinted them by now?'

Bradley put his head in his hands. 'Aw no, what will Charlotte think about that?'

'So Bradley, we will have Sara, Charlotte, Oog, Lucy and Donna coming to Cambridge in the morning. Terry can fix times with them.'

'I'll have a word with Charlotte before she leaves.'

'We need to take statements from the other staff. They've been going back and forth all evening. Which reminds me of our runaway, Elsie.' Silly girl. Why had she run off? Had she seen something that frightened her into running away? 'Can you organise for Terry or Carlos to go and pick her up?'

'Will do. And lastly we have Agnes who is related to a suspect.'

'Yes. Her statement should be interesting.'

'It certainly will be. If she tells us everything.'

Harry flipped open his notebook and unfolded his table plan. He pointed to one name.

''This is my prime suspect at present, Bradley.'

'Really?'

29

WITNESS STATEMENT

Statement of: *Walter Manners*
Age if under 18: *over 18* Occupation: *Lorry driver*

This statement (consisting of 1 page(s) each signed by me) is true to the best of my knowledge and belief and I make it knowing that, if it is tendered in evidence, I shall be liable to prosecution if I have wilfully stated in it anything which I know to be false, or do not believe to be true.
Witness Signature: *wmanners* Date: *07/12/2024*

I am Walter Manners of this parish. I came to the Red Lion because my wife Ida had booked it. I often have to do my bit to prop her up in her council roll and I wasn't out in the truck this evening so I went. The food here was nice but apart from Mick Gotobed who I know from school, there was no one worth talking to.

I did not get up from the table all evening. I did not go to the toilet. We'd only had time to eat our main courses when the trouble kicked in.

If you ask me, Paul Leonard is a flaky sort of person. His wife is a cow. I don't trust her. That's probably why Paul is like he is. I did see him leave the table and we all saw the stupid man trying to get out through the fire exit. Why did he do that? Must be guilty of something. That's what I think anyways.

*****

WITNESS STATEMENT

Statement of: *Jane Gotobed*
Age if under 18: *over 18* Occupation: *Housewife*

This statement (consisting of 1 page(s) each signed by me) is true to the best of my knowledge and belief and I make it knowing that, if it is tendered in evidence, I shall be liable to prosecution if I have wilfully stated in it anything which I know to be false, or do not believe to be true.
Witness Signature: *Jane Gotobed* Date: *07/12/2024*

I am this person. I was sitting with Ida Manners and her husband and my husband and the Leonards. We was having a nice night out. I don't get out so much because I don't drive and John isn't often at home because he works long hours. So this was a treat.

Ida Manners is a friend. I've known her all my life. You can believe what she says. I don't know those people the Leonards. Don't want to know them either. He's shifty. Imagine trying to escape from a nice restaurant? And his wife is snooty, too posh for me.

I didn't leave the table all evening. I hope we can go

home soon. The night is spoiled.

---

* * * * *

WITNESS STATEMENT

Statement of: *Mick Gotobed*
Age if under 18: *over 18* Occupation: *Agricultural*

This statement (consisting of 1 page(s) each signed by me) is true to the best of my knowledge and belief and I make it knowing that, if it is tendered in evidence, I shall be liable to prosecution if I have wilfully stated in it anything which I know to be false, or do not believe to be true.
Witness Signature: *Mick Gotobed* Date: *07/12/2024*

I can't say a lot mate. I stayed at the table all evening. I wouldn't be here only for it's the winter and not so much to do. Jane the wife doesn't get out much because I work long hours and she doesn't drive. She doesn't see her friend Ida much and I'm not sorry about that because the woman is a bit of a bully but they're friends so there and I'd better not say any more about that.

I never met Paul Leonard or his wife before. They were fine. I think both of them went to the toilet. Everyone knows what a fool Paul Leonard made of himself trying to get out of the restaurant. Wally and I had to pull the man away from the fire exit. Imagine if the alarm had gone off? We would have had the fire brigade here and the whole town would have been disrupted. The police were here though and they did take the idiot away so I suppose it was all under control.

And we don't even have to pay for the meal which is

very nice of the owners so I don't understand what he was doing. Hope this helps.

---

* * * * *

WITNESS STATEMENT

Statement of: *Ida Manners (Mrs)*
Age if under 18: *over 18* Occupation: *District Councillor*

This statement (consisting of 1 page(s) each signed by me) is true to the best of my knowledge and belief and I make it knowing that, if it is tendered in evidence, I shall be liable to prosecution if I have wilfully stated in it anything which I know to be false, or do not believe to be true.
Witness Signature: *Ida Manners* Date: *07/12/2024*

I want to say that I think this matter has been handled badly. The police haven't been very helpful and we've had to stay here for a very long time without being told what's going on. I intend to bring this matter up at the next meeting of the District Council.

I am shocked to discover that the Leonards are criminals. I would never have associated with them if I'd known that. I wouldn't have invited my good friend Jane Gotobed and her husband out to dinner if I'd known. It's a dreadful thing. I'm very sorry about the poor woman who's been hurt or killed or something. I can't say for certain what happened to her and that's another matter I intend to complain about. Why wasn't I told?

I know none of us on our table, apart from the Leonards, were involved in that accident. We are good upstanding citizens. Mick and my husband were at school together as were Jane and I. We know each other very well. We are not criminals or wicked people. We should have been let go home long since.

Paul Leonard is an entrepreneur or anyway that's what he told me and he does business in Ely. It was he who recommended this restaurant. I must say the food was good and it was kind of the owners to say we didn't have to pay for our meal. A very sensible choice, I think.

I noticed both Paul Leonard and his wife Kylie leaving the table early on. I sit on the District Council and I have to be observant. I was looking down the room where I was sitting. They weren't the only people who went to the bathroom. I saw that man from the table for four just by the end of the corridor getting up too. I remember that because I know him, Mr Black. A nice man who does a lot of charity work. You can believe what he says. So he went to the bathroom and I saw a woman with bushy frizzy hair going down at the same time. I wondered at the time if they knew each other but Mr Black came back and then Paul Leonard went racing down – honestly, can he have been in such a hurry to get to the toilet? He's a young man. Wait until he gets older and gets prostate trouble like my Wally.

That woman who went down the corridor never returned. I'm sure she didn't because I would have noticed and I didn't. I think now that she must be the person who was hurt or killed or both.

What I want to know is where is the ambulance? I think the police are failing in their duty not getting an ambulance swiftly to help the poor woman. Is that why she died? Maybe it wasn't a killing after all but simply a case of dereliction of duty. I know that there have been terrible delays in people getting ambulances and one of our old folk died the other week waiting for one. We have defibrillators but if it's a bad heart attack nothing helps. The police only had to run up to the football club for a defibrillator.

So it was a pleasant evening until it went wrong. We had to move tables because I didn't want to sit next to a criminal's wife. She's a nasty piece of work anyway. Properly up herself. I can't be seen to be associating with people like that. I have a reputation to maintain. I will not be supporting Kylie Leonard's application for a change of use on the shop she wants to turn into a hair salon. I intend to say my piece at the next planning meeting.

I hope we are soon let go. Jane is getting very tired. She's not used to being out late at night and she had a fall a few weeks ago. It's not right to keep us here.

Bradley picked up the completed statements.

'Can we go now,' asked Ida Manners.

'If you wouldn't mind waiting another few minutes, Mrs Manners. We just need to check through the statements.'

Bradley left the Victorian Room in search of Harry. They read through the papers, marked where Mrs Manners had described when Paul Leonard and Tom Black had moved down the corridor.

Harry went to speak to Mrs Manners. 'Thank you all for your statements. This is very useful. You can all leave now.'

'I should think so too,' said Mrs Manners, whose husband was helping her into her coat.

'We will be in be in touch with you and Mr Gotobed as you both saw Mr Leonard leave the table.'

Harry wondered how the others hadn't seen anything. Still, he had two more witnesses, along with Sara and Tom

Black. They could always get in touch with the others if necessary.

'Yeah mate,' replied Mick Gotobed. 'Anything to help. Just ask. But you'd better phone me on my mobile as I'll be out working. It's a busy time of the year.'

Mrs Manners swept out of the room, followed by her group. Bradley moved quickly to signal to Pete that they could be let go. Thank goodness their fingerprints hadn't been found in the bar or toilets.

30

Mariama told Harry that it was proving difficult to get prints from the lemon cutting knife. It had been washed. She had spotted blood on the blade and in the join between the handle and the blade, so she was hopeful that it would prove to be the murder weapon after full forensics were conducted. 'We'll have to check fingerprints against those we've taken from the bar, especially from the coffee table by the victim, the bar counter, and the worktop at the back of the bar where the plate of cut lemons was kept.'

'So, in theory, we can narrow down our list of suspects after you've finished fingerprinting.'

'In theory. Our mobile device is very accurate, but it's always useful to be cautious.'

Bradley came out to the Incident Van. 'I've let the four from Paul Leonard's table go. None of them went down the corridor. Mr Anstey is sitting at our old table. How's the fingerprinting going?'

'We've processed and eliminated most. We're waiting for results against what we've picked up from the bar.'

'While we're waiting, Bradley,' said Harry, 'why not take a statement from Vi? Has the squad car been sent for Elsie, by the way?'

'We need to free up one of the PCs before we can do that.'

'I thought Carlos was finished?'

'Here I am!' Carlos joined them. 'I was cleaning my hands.'

'Okay. Come with me and I'll get Elsie's address. I've already spoken to her mother who promised to keep her there until we collected her. Pick her up, please and bring her back. Be firm if she tries to get out of returning.'

'Okay, Boss.'

Harry went back to the Victorian Room. Bradley soon joined him.

'Okay, we're down to four. Let's divide them up. Will you speak to Mrs Leonard, when you've taken Vi's statement? I'll speak to Tom Black and his wife. As you've already spoken to Agnes, will you take her on?'

'It will be a pleasure?'

Harry laughed. 'I doubt that. Vi can go if her fingerprints haven't been found in the bar. Ditto for Rochelle and Mr Rouse. I'll tell them they can leave. I want to hold onto Mrs Leonard until we can clear Paul Leonard, or not clear, whatever the case may be. Agnes has a link to them.'

'Okay,' said Bradley. 'I'll tease what I can out of Agnes. We may need to take her into Cambridge, though.'

'Indeed. Depending on what happens with our principal suspects, we may have to take her into Cambridge this evening. We'll pass that delightful task to Carlos.'

31

Sara had run out of small talk. Charlotte's head kept tipping forwards. Poor thing. Oog was the only one of them who looked fresh and alert. His police training, Sara decided. She wondered when they would be let go.

She rubbed at her fingertips. The technician said their fingerprints would not stay on the system if there was no match for what they found in the bar. Rochelle had fussed over having her prints taken. She only agreed when the technician promised they would not be kept on file.

Rochelle and Mr Rouse were openly arguing now.

'This is a great end to what you said was going to be a great night.'

'I'm sorry Rochelle.'

'You said you were going to leave your wife to be with me.'

'That was months ago. Things have changed. I can't leave her now that she's pregnant.'

'You shouldn't have been sleeping with her when you were seeing me. That was cheating.'

Illogical. Sara smiled and shook her head.

Harry came into the room and went over to Rochelle and Mr Rouse. 'You can both go now.'

'About time.' Rochelle jumped up and flounced to the front door. Pete had to leap across and open it.

But once outside, Rochelle came back quickly. 'Who's going to take me home?'

Johnny Rouse had also stood. His clothes seemed to droop on him. 'I'll drive you home,' he said to Rochelle.

Rochelle sniffed and went back out the door.

'I hope you can patch things up with your wife,' said Harry, softly, but Sara overheard.

'Well there's one good thing has come out of this evening. I won't have anything to do with Rochelle again. She's been nasty and difficult.'

And you've been angel? Sara shook her head.

Harry watched them go. 'Two minutes,' he said and went down the corridor.

Apart from Sara, Oog and Charlotte, there were just four other people, left in the Oak Room. Mrs Leonard, Fred Anstey, and Mr and Mrs Black. Sara tried to avoid looking at Fred Anstey. He was obviously bored. He had already tried to engage Tom Back in conversation. Tom had shut that down quickly.

She didn't think Mr Black or his party had given statements yet either.

When could they leave? What an evening. What a disaster. That poor woman.

Sara wished she could have a glass of wine but there was little hope of that. She'd only drunk half her glass of red; the second half was sitting abandoned on the table Mrs Manners had commandeered.

Never mind. There was a bottle of white in the fridge at home. She had been planning to have a glass after work yesterday but by the time she got home, she was too tired to drink alcohol. Arabella had been grumpy because he'd had to wait for fresh food and cuddles. Blasted cat. Still, it would be nice to cuddle up with him on the sofa, with a glass of wine, once she got home. Keeping that thought in her mind, Sara let herself drift back to the room.

Nearly there, she thought.

Oog leaned forward. 'I think almost everyone has been interviewed. We should soon be able to go. Charlotte, are you feeling tired?'

'I am. I could go to sleep on the spot. I so want to go home.'

Harry came back with Bradley who whisked Charlotte away. Harry spoke briefly to Tom Black on his way to the kitchen, saying he wouldn't be long.

'What about me?' whinged Fred Anstey, from the nearby table.

'Stay where you are for the present,' said Harry.

'And what about my husband?' asked Mrs Leonard.

'My colleague will talk to you shortly.'

Harry crossed the room to sit with Sara and Oog.

'You are winding down, Harry?' said Oog.

'Yes. Nearly there now.'

He passed her phone to Sara. ''There you are. We've removed the photos Oog took, and left everything else as it was.'

''Thanks, Harry.' Sara put the phone in her bag.

'You can all go home.'

'Should I call a taxi, Harry?' asked Sara.

'I wondered if you'd like to take my car? You're still on the insurance.'

Oh, thought Sara. I am? Why didn't he take me off?

'But if you don't feel like driving, I'll get a taxi for you, or maybe Pete or Dev could drive you home?'

'No, don't call them away from the work here. I'm happy to drive us back to Cambridge.'

'Are you sure? You look tired.'

Sara's energy had come back now she knew they could leave. 'It's fine. I'll do it.'

Harry drew a bunch of keys from his pocket, separated the car key, and handed it over. 'Text me when you get home. Okay? And I'll call to you in the morning.'

Charlotte came back with Bradley. They collected their coats and left.

32

WITNESS STATEMENT

Statement of: *Vi Marshall*
Age if under 18: *over 18* Occupation: *Sous chef*

This statement (consisting of 1 page(s) each signed by me) is true to the best of my knowledge and belief and I make it knowing that, if it is tendered in evidence, I shall be liable to prosecution if I have wilfully stated in it anything which I know to be false, or do not believe to be true.
Witness Signature: *V Marshall* Date: *07/12/2024*

I am the abovenamed person and I am the sous-chef at the Red Lion. I've been doing that for two years. I was busy all evening because the restaurant was full. I didn't leave the kitchen all evening. Neither did Lucy. I heard Agnes, especially, talking, but you'll be speaking to her. There's no point in me talking about stuff that's hearsay. That's all I know.

* * * * *

WITNESS STATEMENT

Statement of: *Agnes Leonard*
Age if under 18: *over 18*
Occupation: *Waitress at The Red Lion*

This statement (consisting of 2 page(s) each signed by me) is true to the best of my knowledge and belief and I make it knowing that, if it is tendered in evidence, I shall be liable to prosecution if I have wilfully stated in it anything which I know to be false, or do not believe to be true.
Witness Signature: *Agnes Leonard* Date: *07/12/2024*

I am the abovenamed Agnes Leonard. I work a few days a week at the Red Lion. I've been doing that for more than two years. I was serving in the Victorian Room this evening. There was a big group in there. Donna helped me when we were serving the dinners as we had twenty to hand out and everyone wanted to have their dinner at the same time. No patience.

I've been working hard all evening but I saw a lot going on. I knew when Donna and Lucy kept going missing that it was something serious. The handsome policeman, Harry, was trying to keep things from me but I wasn't born yesterday. I know the regulars and I joke and laugh with them and I pick things up. I tried to find out what was going on but I never suspected that it would be a murder.

That woman in the bar who was killed? I never met her. I absolutely don't believe that my cousin Paul Leonard would hurt a fly. He's a lovely man and so soft-hearted. His wife isn't like him but she's my cousin by marriage so I won't hear a word said against her. I'm sure that drunken man from the group in the Victorian Room must have killed the dead woman.

The only other person I saw going down the corridor was Tom Black. I know him. My dad worked for him and I did summer work in his potato sheds years ago. Back-breaking work it was. People go on about how hard waitressing is. Vi, when she was doing it and Elsie moan about it. They should try grading potatoes. That's a crap job. And when the potatoes are rotten they sure stink. I'd much rather work in a nice restaurant where there are always delicious smells and the clients are interesting people and they tip well.

Of course I understand that someone killed the woman in the bar but I'm sure it was that man from her own group. I overheard the women saying that drunk guy with the Young Farmers group met her on a dating app. You have to be so careful these days. I always swipe left if I see something I don't like in a guy's eyes. That woman should have been more careful.

I've been very helpful to the police this evening. I know Paul fainted when he saw the dead woman because I overheard what was going on. The police should know that only an innocent man would faint when he saw a dead body. My cousin did not kill that woman.

33

Sara, Charlotte and Oog walked around to the carpark. Sara sat into Harry's car and adjusted the seat so that she could move it further forward. She did it almost unconsciously, because it had always been necessary to change where the setting was when she had borrowed Harry's car in the past. Charlotte was beside her and Oog sat in the back. It was better that Charlotte was in the front and Sara appreciated Oog's sensitivity in leaving them together.

'Where do you live, Charlotte?'

'Just off Mill Road, on Catherine Street. Do you know where it is?'

'I know Mill Road and I think Catherine Street is the far side of the railway bridge from the city centre. Am I right?'

'Yes.'

'Okay. If I drive in to Newmarket Road and onto the Ring Road will I get to it?'

'Yes, just a bit further on from there. I'll direct you when we get to the big Sainsburys.'

When Sara had connected the SatNav to help her get back to Cambridge, she found her address had been keyed in as a favourite. That gave her a warm glow, warm like the embers of the fire at the Red Lion, which might be fanned into life to start a new fire.

She was glad to be occupied finding her way back to Cambridge. She still had a nagging feeling that she had forgotten something. What could it be? She tried to push the thought from her mind. Best to keep the events of the evening at bay until she was on her own. Oog was quiet in the back, Charlotte was equally so in the front.

But flashes from the evening kept breaking in. She saw again the lovely happy place that she and Harry had walked into. She remembered the tentative feeling of joy on being with him. She shook her head to loosen the memory and concentrated on the road.

The wind had died down completely. Storm Darragh had vanished. They sped along the A14 and before too long, Sara was navigating the narrow Catherine Street. Charlotte directed her almost to the end. Sara stopped the car in the middle of the road because there was nowhere else to stop. Cars were parked on both sides.

'Thanks, Sara. What's your number?' Charlotte thumbed in the digits and Sara heard her own mobile beep. 'Let's keep in touch.'

'Yes,' said Sara. 'Good night.'

Sara turned to ask Oog if he'd like to sit in the front, but he was already slipping into Charlotte's vacated seat.

'Sara,' he said, 'We will go to your place and I will get a taxi to St Benedict's. I don't like you to be driving alone after this evening and the murder. It would not be good for you.'

Sara was going to protest, but the sense of relief that she would not have to drive firstly to St Benedict's and then home, stopped her. Oog would be fine in a taxi. She was desperately tired now. Mentally, her mind was buzzing in all directions. *Go home*, she said to herself. Let Oog come in and they could call a taxi, and she would offer him a drink, because she sure needed one, and they might talk a little while they waited for his ride, discuss the evening.

And then, from nowhere, she remembered what she'd forgotten. She'd told Harry who she had seen going down the corridor, fair enough, but one person had actually gone down the corridor twice. She was sure of it.

'Oog, I have to contact Harry. I've just remembered something important.'

Still stopped in the middle of Catherine Street, Sara phoned Harry but he didn't pick up. She texted him.

* * * * *

Arabella was as charming as ever, which meant the cat hissed at Oog. His fur stuck out straight in all directions and his tail whipped back and forth. Oog stood, looking unsure whether to sit or to leave the room.

'Take no notice of him, Oog. I'm always apologising for the way he treats guests. He's a grumpy cat and that's never going to change.'

'Well, Sara, I'm glad to learn that he is not the female cat because I would not like to see a lovely Arabella behaving so badly.'

They laughed about the cat, who soon ignored Oog and sidled up to Sara. She had knelt down to the fire, which was always set and ready to light. The glow of a warm flaming fire was so soothing.

'What would you like to drink, Oog? Wine? I have white in the fridge, and reds in the cupboard, or would you prefer a whisky, brandy or cognac?'

'But the taxi, Sara?'

'Give it a few minutes. Let's relax before you head off.'

'*Merci.* A cognac, *s'il vous plaît.*'

Oog sat in an armchair by the fire. Sara sat on the sofa. Arabella hopped up onto her lap. They sipped their drinks in a silence broken by the hissing and snapping of wood, and soon, by the sound of Arabella's purring which grew louder and louder as Sara stroked him.

'What an evening,' said Sara, eventually. 'Not what I expected at all.'

'*Mais non.* It is very sad that a person has been killed, but this is the badness in human nature.'

'I've never seen Harry in action before. It felt quite strange. I'm usually, I have usually been, on the edges of his investigations.'

Oog tilted his glass and swirled the contents around the balloon shape. 'Yes, I understand. He is a careful policeman, your Harry.'

Sara's eyes widened at Harry being called hers.

Oog tilted his head and peered at her. Sara would have to be careful. This man was a detective too. He would be a keen observer.

'Yes,' he said, 'I call him your Harry. In the little time that I have known him, I see that he becomes quiet when your name it is mentioned, Sara. But tonight, with you close by, he has been a different person. He admires you, *chèrie*, and more, he trusts you. That was a lot he asked you to do this evening when you are not part of the police. Did you know he has not been at work for a while?'

'Yes, I heard he'd been injured. His arm?'

'He got stabbed.'

'Poor Harry.'

'This evening he managed well.'

Sara longed to see Harry. She could not discuss her secret feelings, the hurt, with anyone else. Except her mother. She suddenly remembered the dead woman. Her heart lurched in her chest. If anything happened to her mother, Sara didn't know how she would bear it. But her mother was safe in Devon. She would phone her in the morning. She would go down and see Mum very soon.

Sara realised she hadn't responded to Oog. Her thoughts were all over the place. Much of that was down to tiredness.

'I will phone for the taxi now, Sara.'

Bless his thoughtfulness. I have misjudged this man. It's nice to have a better opinion of him.

When Oog left, Sara messaged Harry.

> Safely back. Did you get my text? I dropped Charlotte off. Oog insisted that I drive home and he organised a taxi for himself. We had a drink. Arabella hissed at him. Everything normal here!

> Still at RL. Glad you got back safely. Yes I got your text. That information fits. Will phone tomorrow and arrange to pick up car. Thank you for your valuable help this evening. I do want to talk to you but let's get the formal statement out of the way first. Go to bed, you must be exhausted. Good night. X

34

WITNESS STATEMENT

Statement of: *Thomas Andrew Black*
Age if under 18: *over 18*
Occupation: *Owner, agricultural business*

This statement (consisting of 3 page(s) each signed by me) is true to the best of my knowledge and belief and I make it knowing that, if it is tendered in evidence, I shall be liable to prosecution if I have wilfully stated in it anything which I know to be false, or do not believe to be true.
Witness Signature: *Thomas A Black* Date: *07/12/2024*

I am the abovenamed person. I came to Red Lion for dinner this evening. The wife and I often come here with friends, as it's the best food place around. I own and run an agricultural business a couple of miles out of Soham on the road to Ely.

Our table was at the restaurant end of the corridor and I was sitting facing the dresser which is the greeting point for new arrivals. I saw everyone who came and went, whether up or down the corridor. The toilets are down there. I saw the heads of people who were sitting in the Victorian Room – a lovely dining area behind the fireplace and where I've often sat for Sunday lunch. I also saw anyone who went up and down the corridor, including Donna and the waitresses.

I went down the corridor early on. I have prostate trouble and had to get to the toilet in a hurry. A lovely woman came out of the Victorian Room at the same time and we almost collided. I would normally have given way to her but I simply had to get to the toilet. I wish I could apologise to her but I believe she is the woman who was hurt. The least I can do now is give an accurate description of what I saw and hope it's helpful to the police.

I missed seeing anything while I was in the toilet, but I was in there for no more than a couple of minutes at most. When I came out, I overheard an argument going on in the bar. One of the voices was a woman's. I think now it must be the woman I almost bumped into. The argument grew more heated. I couldn't make out most of it out, but I did hear the woman saying something was over. I presumed that she and the man were having a relationship fight. I went away because I don't like poking my nose into something that's not my business. I had only sat down when a youngish man came back to the main dining room. I thought he was wiping tears from his eyes, but I can't swear to that. I watched him go to a table at the far end of the room – the Oak Room, that is. I know the young man. His name is Paul Leonard and I see that he's here with his wife, Kylie.

A little later, I saw a woman go along, I presumed to the toilet. It was Kylie Leonard. She is thin and is wearing a glittery slinky Christmas dress this evening. I'm sure you already know who she is. It was a while before she came back. I noticed her face because although she is young, there are lots of lines on it. Perhaps she's a smoker. My sister was one and now she has more lines on her face than the approach to Euston station. Mrs Leonard went back to the same table as her husband. I looked at them. He didn't speak to his wife, which I thought was odd. He sat there staring out the window.

After that, I mostly noticed the waitresses. I know one of them, Agnes Leonard, by sight. Her father used to work for me. She's a pleasant girl. Donna, of course goes up and down a lot. Later, the policeman, Harry Meredith (I met him before) went down with Donna. I knew something was wrong at that point because Donna was upset. Then the younger policeman from the table behind me, Detective Sergeant Bradley West, was called away with Inspector Meredith. A little while later, Donna brought Geoffrey Norman down the corridor. I know Geoffrey because he's a farmer and we've done business. I can't imagine what they wanted with him. He's a good sort.

So there were a lot of comings and goings up and down the corridor.

I hope this is helpful. I'm happy to answer any questions from the police.

35

Harry and Bradley sat in the Victorian Room. The bundle of statements was laid out into three lots. They were sifting through the latest bunch.

'Agnes can go, Bradley, providing her fingerprints don't match any in the bar.'

'She might have been working there, Harry, getting drinks.'

'I didn't check that with Donna.'

'I'll go and ask. You carry on reading the statements.'

Harry put Agnes's statement aside while he waited for Bradley to return. He began to read Tom Black's.

'No,' said Bradley, sitting back down beside Harry. 'Donna does the drinks in the bar. Agnes shouldn't have been there. Mariama says they didn't find Agnes's prints.'

Harry smiled and shook his head. 'I'm certain she went in. She knows that Natasha Poole is dead. How did she know? We'll have to interview her. We can leave her statement aside for now.'

'Definitely.'

'Okay, looks like you've read Tom Black's statement.

Interesting, isn't it?'

'Let's hold off on Tom Black too,' said Harry. 'He's a more important witness than we realised. Vi can leave now. I doubt Agnes will want to depart in a hurry. She likes knowing things and we're not at the end yet, so just say nothing to her.'

Bradley smiled.

'We're narrowing things down. We'll hang onto Paul Leonard and his wife. We need her statement. Will you sort that when this room is free, Bradley?'

'Sure. Of the remainder, Fred Anstey doesn't look like he's a serious suspect. He didn't go down the corridor until after the body was found.'

'No, and Mariama can't find his fingerprints in the bar. We can eliminate him as a suspect but I want him to come to Cambridge for an interview tomorrow. He's important because of his connection to Natasha.'

Bradley stood to clear away the statements. He rolled them up and put them in a pocket.

'I'll go to the kitchen, Bradley, and then have a word with Mariama. When I get back to the Oak Room, I'll speak to Tom Black. You can bring Mrs Leonard in here. I'll speak to Mr Anstey and let him go.'

Bradley took Mrs Leonard into the Victorian Room, leaving Mr Anstey under the watchful eye of Pete. Harry went down to the bar to catch up with Mariama and the technicians.

'We have four people left, Mariama, the Leonards, Tom and Mrs Black, and Mr Anstey. Let's focus on Anstey. What have you found?'

'As I said, there isn't a match for Mr Anstey's fingerprints. Of course we can't eliminate him completely, but given the forensics, he's a low-level suspect.'

'Good, I'll release him. What about the others?'

'Paul Leonard's prints are on the coffee table but nowhere else. He was definitely close to the body. We can't rule him out as having handled the knife because a deeper analysis than we can perform here must be done on that.'

'And Mrs Leonard?'

'Nothing. No prints anywhere, neither in the toilets, nor anywhere else.'

'But she was in the corridor. Nothing on the door handles?'

'Nothing.'

'What did she do? She was knocking on doors.'

'I can't help you there. I know you saw her but the lack of fingerprint evidence suggests she wasn't in the bar or the toilets.'

'She must have wiped the surfaces down.'

'That would be my guess,' said Mariama. 'And there's no trace of Mr Black's prints. You'll need to establish if he went to the toilet after Mrs Leonard.'

* * * * *

Harry returned to the restaurant. 'You can go,' he said to Fred Anstey. 'But hold yourself ready to come to Cambridge in the morning. You'll get a call arranging a time for you give a formal statement.'

Fred Anstey stood. He was still a little unsteady. 'But how am I to get home? Natasha drove me here. She was the driver. What am I to do?'

'Pete,' said Harry, turning to the constable. 'Will you call a taxi for Mr Anstey.'

Harry turned away and went into the Victorian Room.

Kylie Leonard was sitting across the table from Bradley. She stood as he entered the room. 'Can I go now?

I've told you all I know. Where's my husband?'

'Please sit down, Mrs Leonard.'

Harry picked up her statement. He studied the single sheet of sparse writing.

WITNESS STATEMENT

Statement of: *Kylie Leonard*
Age if under 18: *over 18*
Occupation: *Beautician Hairdresser*

This statement (consisting of 1 page(s) each signed by me) is true to the best of my knowledge and belief and I make it knowing that, if it is tendered in evidence, I shall be liable to prosecution if I have wilfully stated in it anything which I know to be false, or do not believe to be true.
Witness Signature: *K Leonard* Date: *07/12/2024*

I am the abovenamed person. I work full time. My husband Paul and I came out with friends for dinner this evening.

I left my table to go to the toilet. I came straight back to my table. I never went to the bar. I never met the woman who had an accident. My husband only left the table to go to the toilet and he came straight back. That's all I know.

'Okay Mrs Leonard. Let's start again.' Harry sat down.

'I want to leave. I've told you what I know. You can't keep me here. I didn't do anything.' She stood and began moving around the end of the table to the exit.

Harry reached it ahead of her. 'Sit back down, Mrs Leonard.' What he wouldn't give for a nice secure interview room. Perhaps he should just take her back to

Cambridge. After all, her husband was going there regardless.

She stood in front of Harry, arms crossed, eyes blazing. 'I'm waiting for you to move,' she said.

Harry almost laughed. The woman's attitude reminded him of Agnes, although the pair were only related by marriage. 'Sit back down, Mrs Leonard.'

She continued to stand and tried to stare him down. It was rare for a woman to be so aggressive, but Harry could be patient.

After a while, Kylie Leonard pulled out a chair and sat facing the French doors.

'Sit at the top of the table, please,' said Harry.

He didn't want her making a dash for it. Neither did he want her to see them moving her husband from the Function Room, which was visible through the French doors.

Bradley drew a chair out for her and sat on her left side. Harry picked a chair on her right. They boxed her in.

Harry had picked up Mrs Leonard's statement. He placed it on the table in front of her.

'Shall we start again?'

'I told you I have nothing more to add.' She sat, hands on the table. Her painted nails tapped the wood. She flashed angry looks at Harry.

'If you cooperate, Mrs Leonard, we can get this interview over quickly. What time did you go to the toilet?'

'I can't remember. Where is my husband? I insist on seeing my husband.'

'That won't be possible, just now. He's helping us with our enquiries.'

Harry thought he saw a flicker of fear in the woman's eyes. It was hard to be sure.

'Try to remember when you went to the toilet, Mrs Leonard.'

'But I can't! We were eating and talking and I didn't check my watch when I went to the loo. For goodness sake!'

'We've taken statements from the people at your table,' said Bradley.' We may be able to narrow down the times you and your husband were away from your party.'

'I doubt that. Ida Manners talks so much I'm surprised she remembers her own name. Besides, she was busy eating eating eating. It was disgusting. I couldn't bear to watch. No wonder she's as big as the side of a house.'

Kylie Leonard had begun waving her hands as she spoke. Harry noticed the black fingerprinting ink on her thumb. He thought there was a dash of red there too.

Mrs Leonard saw him looking. She put her hands under the table. 'You won't get much out of them anyway. They all follow where Mrs Bad Manners leads.'

'Your husband left the table before you,' said Harry. 'We have two witnesses who saw him. They also saw you heading down the corridor immediately after your husband sat back down.'

'I'd been on my own with that lot. I was desperate for a pee and a fag.' Her feet were tapping the floor.

'So you went to the toilet?'

'I already said I did!'

'Which one?'

'The, the, eh, the first one.'

'Good,' said Harry. 'We should find your fingerprints there. Where did you go to smoke? It's not allowed in the restaurant.'

The tempo of Kylie Leonard's foot-tapping increased. 'I never touch anything in a public toilet. I don't want to catch nasty bugs.' She lowered her head and mumbled. 'I didn't actually smoke.'

'And you used the first toilet? The first one along the

corridor?'

'No, I, em, I used the disabled toilet. No one ever goes in there so it's the cleanest.'

The toilet where Oog had found the knife which had been inserted into a decorative barrel on the window sill.

'Did you wash your hands?'

Once again, Harry was treated to a venomous look.

'Of course I washed my hands.'

'So we will find fingerprints on the tap.'

'I always wipe everything down. I'm a tidy person.'

'Did you go to the bar,' asked Bradley, as the woman was staring at Harry.

She flipped her head around. 'I, I… I told you I only went to the toilet.'

'So you didn't go to the bar,' said Harry.

'No!' She spat the word out at such a rate that spittle came with it. Harry leaned back. He'd had good practice in doing that during the Covid pandemic, when angry suspects thought they could intimidate the police by infecting them with the virus.

It was obvious the woman wasn't going to talk. They would have to take her and her husband to Cambridge and question them in formal surroundings. Doubtless, Mrs Leonard would insist on a solicitor. Harry and Bradley were very lucky to have obtained the information they had received from the restaurant customers and staff, without someone calling for legal representation.

Harry went out to the Oak Room. PC Pete was still warming his backside at the almost dead fire. 'Pete, have you got your cuffs?'

Pete pulled a set from the back of his belt.

'Cuff Mrs Leonard, please. She's in the Victorian Room with Bradley. Then help Bradley to get her upstairs.'

Harry waited for Pete to return and continue guard

duties, then he went down to the bar.

Mariama was there. 'Got a suspect?' she asked.

'Got three, as it happens.'

'Three of them?'

'Yep, three suspects but only one killer.'

36

Harry headed back to the kitchen.

Lucy and Donna were the only occupants. They were resting their elbows on the now clean work surface. A dishwasher was humming away in the anteroom.

'We're almost done,' he said.

'Do you know who the killer is?' asked Lucy.

'We think so. We're taking three suspects back to Cambridge with us.'

'Three? Can we know who they are?' asked Donna.

'I don't see why not. You'll spot who they are as we put them in the patrol cars. It's Paul Leonard, his wife Kylie, and Tom Black.'

'The Leonards? Agnes's cousins? You've got to be joking.' Donna had straightened up. 'And Tom Black? Tom Black!'

'Are you making a mistake, Harry?' asked Lucy.

'Tom had a very good view of everyone who moved up and down the corridor. We want to get closer detail from him. The Leonards have been acting suspiciously. Keep that information to yourselves, please. We have work to do before we can be certain who the killer is.'

'And will you let us know when it's confirmed?'

Harry watched Lucy and Donna move closer to each other. They were a good team. They would doubtless help each other come to terms with the events of the evening.

'I will. Has Elsie been brought back?'

'Not yet. Oh wait, I can see the squad car coming into the car park.'

'Right. More work to be done.'

'Go gently with her, Harry,' said Donna. 'She's quite timid.'

Harry left the kitchen and went across to the Function Room. It was the first time he'd been in the building. The sense of space surprised him. It had large arched windows and a vaulted ceiling. Long tables were spread the length of the room.

Paul Leonard was sitting at one of the tables, his back to the windows. He had long since come out of his faint. Dev was keeping an eye on him although the man was still handcuffed. It was very cold in the building. Harry guessed that, as it wasn't being used, it wasn't heated. Dev seemed to be coping with the low temperature, but Paul Leonard was shivering.

'Did you have a jacket or coat?' he asked, sitting opposite the man.

'Yeah. Navy-blue three-quarter length.'

'Will you get that, please Dev?'

'Have you recovered from your faint?'

'Yeah. Silly that. It was such a shock though, seeing her there.' Paul Leonard looked away from Harry, lowered his head into his hands and sobbed.

Dev returned with the coat. He stood by the man until his sobbing subsided, removed the handcuffs and passed the coat to him.

'Thanks, mate.' Paul Leonard shrugged into the coat and sat back down. He rubbed a hand under his nose. Dev took a handkerchief from a pocket and handed it over.

'Thanks, mate.'

Leonard began crying in earnest. Perhaps Dev's act of kindness had set him off. 'S…s… sorry,' he hiccupped. 'It's just such… such a shock. I can't believe she's dead. I only saw her a little while ago.'

'How long have you known Natasha?' asked Harry.

'A long while, six months, maybe more.'

'How well did you know her?'

'We were having,' he sniffed, 'an, an affair.' He looked up suddenly. 'My wife doesn't know. Natasha ended it two weeks ago. I couldn't get her to change her mind. She said she was putting the affair behind her. She, she'd heard I was married.' Paul Leonard laid his head in his hands. 'I should have told her sooner. I should have.'

Harry found himself feeling sorry for the man. *There but for the grace of God go I*, he thought. His brief affair with Maria came back vividly, how intense it had been in the beginning, how quickly it had faded. He hadn't told Maria about Sara. Harry felt like an idiot.

Paul Leonard began talking again. 'I saw her come into the restaurant this evening. She was with some bloke. It was like a kick in the stomach. I wanted to get her back. I had to see her. But I was there with my wife and some friends of hers. How would I manage to speak to Natasha?'

Harry was jotting down what Paul Leonard was saying.

'It was all I was thinking of while the others were eating and drinking. I couldn't touch a bite.' He sniffed, blew into Dev's handkerchief. 'I texted her, Natasha, but the message didn't go through. She'd blocked me!' He shook his head as though he still found the fact unbelievable.

'What did you do?' asked Harry.

'I saw her come out of the other room like I said. She looked so lovely. Her hair was tied at her neck but it fluffed around her head like a halo. I've never been so much in love in my entire life, mate. I had to see her. She turned down the corridor which leads to the toilets and the bar. I jumped out of my seat. Kylie, the wife, stared at me. *Gotta take a piss*, I said to her. She stared. *What?* she said but I just headed off. Natasha must have been in the toilet. I stood in the bar entrance, waiting for her to come out. Then I called her name.'

He stopped talking. Was he reliving what had happened? Harry waited, then asked, And then?'

'She looked surprised, but I know she was pleased to see me. There was no one in the bar so we sat down on the sofa, where… where she was—' He closed his eyes, covered them with his fingers, rocked backwards and forwards on the chair.

In the silence, Harry called up an image of the dead woman. Yes, he thought, she would have been lovely. 'How long were you in the bar with her?'

'I don't know, I can't remember. Seeing her again, it was overwhelming. I touched her hair, kissed her.'

'Did she try to stop you?'

'No. I know she loved me. I tried to persuade her to change her mind. But she said we shouldn't be doing this, that it was over. We started arguing. I said we should get back together again, she said no, that I had a wife. I told her I was going to leave my wife. But still she wouldn't change her mind. She pushed me away, said the age difference was a problem, that the relationship would go sour eventually. I p-pleaded with her to change her mind.'

Once again, the man fell silent.

Harry gave him a few moments, then asked, 'How old are you Mr Leonard?'

'Thirty-one,' he sighed.

'She was a fair bit older, wasn't she?'

'Yeah. But it made no difference. I was mad for her. She was so gorgeous, so much fun. She… I can't believe she's dead.' He began weeping into the handkerchief again.

'Mr Leonard,' said Harry. 'We'll have to take you to the station in Cambridge.'

'Yeah, mate. Take me anywhere, anywhere, as long as it's away from here.'

37

Agnes was clearing away when Harry went to talk to Tom Black. Tom's wife, Pammy, was sitting at Harry's old table in one of the Winchester chairs. Tom still sat at their original table.

'You didn't leave with your friends, Mrs Black?' asked Harry.

'No sir, no. I wanted to stay here with Tom.'

Tom stood up. 'There was no need to stay, Pammy. Everything is fine. I'll get a taxi for you.'

'No, I'm staying with you, Tom.'

Pammy pushed herself up off the chair. Harry thought the woman looked very unwell. She stayed leaning over the table, her hands palm down, as though they were helping her to stay upright. He wondered how to ask her for a statement without upsetting her further.

'You need to let Tom go, Inspector. Tom's a good man. He's been good to me.'

'The Inspector will let me go in a minute, Pammy. Don't distress yourself.'

Agnes plonked her loaded tray onto the table, missing

one of Pammy's fingers by inches. Harry was on the point of telling her to go the kitchen when Pammy spoke again.

'He didn't do it, you have to let him go, Inspector.'

'Didn't do what, Mrs Black?'

'Pammy, stop talking,' hissed Tom, 'you're working yourself into a state.'

'I worry so.'

She looked more angry than worried, Harry thought. She reminded him of his nephew who gave what Harry called 'evils' to his mum when he didn't get his way.

So what might Mrs Black want? What was Tom denying her?

Pammy Black was in her fifties, he thought. Late fifties. There was a huge contrast between her and the lovely, but deceased, Natasha. From what he remembered of a former meeting with Tom and Mrs Black, which would have been two years ago, she had put on a lot of weight.

Harry remembered her as being cheerful. What had changed her? She had barely nodded when he said hello earlier in the evening. If she was unhappy, what was causing that unhappiness? There was more going on here than met the eye.

How would he separate her from Tom so that he could speak to her privately? And he needed to get rid of Agnes.

Agnes slowly squeezed the cutlery onto her overfull tray. Harry could see she was determined to hang around. He was on the point of finding Donna, when she came through the kitchen door.

'Have you finished in here, Agnes?'

'Nearly.'

'Oh Tom, Pammy. I didn't realise you were still here. Let me get your coats.'

'No I have to stay,' said Pammy.

'Go home, Pammy.' Tom urged again.

Harry felt more like an observer than an actor in the scene. He decided to let things play out.

'I can't go!' Tears began dripping down her face. 'I wish you'd never met her, I do.'

'Shut up, Pammy.' Tom jumped up and stood between his wife and Harry.

Agnes moved a little back but still hovered close to the table.

'Well I do! I wish I'd stayed sitting in the outside chair. Then you wouldn't have been able to use that prostate trick. I would have refused to move when I saw her come out of the other dining room.'

Tom moved closer to his wife, took her arm. 'You need to go home, Pammy. Now! I'll call a taxi.'

The colour that Donna had recovered was draining away from her face. 'I, I… Will I order a taxi, Harry?'

Agnes dropped a knife.

Before Harry could intervene, Pammy tried to pull away from Tom who only gripped her arm more tightly.

'I won't go.' She squealed. 'I won't go. You'll start lying again.'

'Stand away from your wife, Tom.' Harry put his hand on Tom's shoulder and tried to draw him away from his wife. 'Pete! he called.

Pete ran across and grabbed hold of the now struggling man. Agnes snatched up a cup and flung it at Tom. Her aim missed.

'You filthy liar. My cousin is getting arrested for murder and it was you all along. It was you! You mean lying bastard.'

38

'Take Agnes away, please Donna.'

Donna clutched Agnes firmly by the arm and marched her off to the kitchen.

Harry motioned Bradley and Pete to take Tom into the Victorian Room.

Harry moved the tray to another table and sat with Pammy Black. She was sobbing. He waited until the sobbing eased.

'Tell me what's going on, Pammy.'

'It wasn't her fault. I don't blame the woman. They told me – the ones in Tom's office – that he was always after her. She left to get away, they said.'

'Natasha Poole worked for Tom?'

'Yes. I've been sitting here thinking back over things and the strange way Tom has behaved. Oh it breaks my heart, that my own husband, the father of my children, could do such a thing.'

Pammy's breath was coming in gasps now. It caught and she began hyperventilating. Harry worried they might actually need the ambulance which had come to take away

Natasha Poole's body.

He ran to the kitchen and fetched a glass of water. Donna, Lucy and Agnes stared but he dashed off before they could speak.

'Here you are.' He pushed the glass into Pammy's hands, and held it until she put her fingers around it. She drank. Her breathing calmed.

'It's okay. I'll be fine now. I'm sorry to be causing trouble for everyone. Sorry for coming here. I thought he was over her. He hadn't been going out so much.' She sipped more water. 'I felt sick when I saw her walk in. I sensed Tom sitting up straight beside me. I wish I'd stayed in the outside chair.'

'What difference would that have made, Pammy?'

'He lies about having prostate trouble. It's an excuse to get away from people. I knew he was going to see her. But he came back. But…'

'He went down the corridor again, didn't he?'

Harry had picked up Sara's message before coming to talk to Pammy and Tom. Sara said she had seen Tom Black go down the corridor twice, not once. The last piece of the puzzle had slotted into place.

'Yes. He was seeing her. But, but to kill her? How could he do that? I've known Tom all my life. I never imagined him being a killer.' She blew her nose. 'I'll have to keep a close eye on the children now. Tom was a good man once. I know that young man he followed down the corridor. That's Paul Leonard. His wife is a hairdresser. I saw him with Natasha a month or so back. Maybe Tom did too. It was jealousy. Tom's always liked to have his own way. Jealousy. That must have been why.'

Pammy began crying again. Harry sat back. After a while, he leaned across the table and patted her arm.

'Thanks for talking to me, Pammy. You'll have to give

a statement. I'll need you to come to Cambridge. I'm really sorry about this.'

'It's not your fault, Harry,' she said, looking up at him. Her face was red and blotchy. 'Tom did this terrible thing and he will have to shoulder the blame. I don't know what our children will make of it.'

39

Oog received the expected call from Harry early the following morning, asking him to come to the station and give a statement.

'It's been a long night, Oog. We called out extra squad cars in the end and took six people back to Cambridge for interviewing.'

'Six! *Vraiment.*'

'Come and see me when you've given your statement. I'll explain what happened after you left The Red Lion.'

*****

'Come in,' called Harry when Oog knocked at his door. He stood to shake hands. 'I hope you're none the worse for what happened last night?'

'I have much enjoyed being involved in the investigation, Harry. It had made the study I do here more valuable. Now I have been involved in working on a real crime in the UK. Yes, some things are the same in Paris as here, but the methods and the challenges, they were not at all like in France.'

Harry smiled. There is nothing amusing about a murder, but Oog's enthusiasm was refreshing.

Harry drew up a spare chair to sit by Oog. 'I really appreciate the help you gave us, Oog. You were invaluable because we were so short of manpower. That is one of the most challenging cases I've been involved in. The crime was as much a shock to us as it was to the innocent diners.'

'And the guilty, Harry?'

'It was clearly murder. Sourcing the knife and stabbing the victim may not have been pre-planned, but it was a deliberate act.'

'And have you found the killer?'

'We're waiting on forensic evidence before we make a formal charge.'

'You are still holding Monsieur and Madame Leonard?'

'No.'

'*Non*? *Quelle surprise*! But Harry, who is it that committed the murder?'

'We let Paul Leonard go fairly soon after arriving back in Cambridge. His fingerprints were only found on the coffee table. There was nothing on the knife.'

Oog nodded. '*Bon*, yes, this I can believe. He was distraught about the dead woman so he would not have killed her. And Madame Leonard?'

'Mrs Leonard refused to talk to us. We found a trace of her blood on the knife. She insisted on having a solicitor with her.'

'But that is sensible for a criminal, *non*?'

'It would be if you were a criminal in need of representation. It was only when we told her that her husband had been released that she finally told us the truth.'

'The truth? And what was that, Harry?'

'Mrs Leonard went to confront Natasha Poole after her husband returned to their table. She walked into the bar and found the woman's body. She thought her husband had killed Natasha Poole. Mrs Leonard went into the disabled toilet to 'catch her breath', as she said, and spotted the knife through the empty spout of the ceramic barrel in the disabled toilet. Realising it could be the murder weapon, she gave it a good wash. Mrs Leonard knew about her husband's affair, and that it had ended. She cleaned the knife to protect her husband.'

'Ah, where I found the lemon-cutting knife? It was well-hidden. This woman, she is cold.'

'She was calm throughout, until Bradley asked if she'd been to the bar. She really gave herself away then.'

'*Mais non*! And Monsieur Leonard? He has recovered?'

'I don't think he'll ever recover from what happened to Natasha Poole. It's one thing to break up with someone you love as deeply as he must have loved the victim, but the horror of seeing her dead and realising that she was murdered, that his affair with her probably led to her death – that may never leave him.'

'And so Mrs Leonard, she is innocent?'

'We wondered initially if it was Mrs Leonard, but on checking through all the witness statements, it became clear that one person was lying to us.'

'But who?' asked Oog, leaning forward.

'Sara messaged me when she got to Cambridge. She remembered that she had seen our principle suspect going down the corridor twice.'

'*Ah oui*, I was in the car with the lovely Sara. But she did not tell me what the message was about.'

'We're still waiting for forensic confirmation but we have a statement from the man's wife which incriminates him. He, I'm talking about Tom Black, refuses to talk.'

'Monsieur Black? *Vraiment*? But he was sitting beside us! *Mon Dieu*! How did this happen?'

'He left his table twice to go to the toilet, allegedly.'

'But Harry, he has the prostate trouble!'

'His wife says he doesn't. It seems he uses it as an excuse to get away from people or out of things. When he said to the other people at their table that he needed the toilet, and trotted out the usual excuse, Mrs Black became suspicious. She had seen Natasha Poole. He went down the corridor twice, which made her doubly suspicious.'

'Did Sara see him go down the corridor?'

'She did, but more than that, Elsie, the waitress, actually saw him go into the bar. She overheard him talking, or rather rowing, with Natasha.'

Oog whistled. 'It is all so sad, *n'est ce pas*?'

Harry's phone rang. Oog sat quietly as Harry murmured replies and thanks. 'Well that's it,' he said, putting the phone down. 'The last two pieces of the jigsaw. Forensics found particles of two blood types on the knife, Natasha Poole's and Kylie Leonard's. There was blood in the junction of the blade with the handle. I thought I spotted blood on Mrs Leonard's thumb when we were interviewing her at the Red Lion. She must have nicked herself when cleaning the knife and it had begun to bleed again. But that's academic now because they also found a partial print on the knife. It's Tom Black's.'

Oog's eyes were growing larger and larger.

'Mrs Black told us Natasha Poole worked briefly at Tom's premises a couple of years ago. Black became fixated on her. We believe the feeling wasn't returned though he continued to contact her. The murder at the Red Lion was the final straw for Mrs Black. She knew he was lying and realised he was the most likely killer. It seems he flipped when he overheard Natasha and Paul

Leonard talking. Once Paul went back to the restaurant, Tom Black took his chance to speak to the dead woman. The stabbing was probably done in the heat of the moment. We found a set of his prints in the bar area and another on the side of the coffee table.'

'*L'amour et la jalouse*!'

'Yes, love and jealousy. Our old friends when it comes to murder.'

Oog stood, ready to depart.

Harry rose also and put his hand out. 'Thank you again, Hugues. If you ever want help in Paris, you know who to call.'

'I do, Harry. It will not be Ghostbusters.' They went out onto the landing, laughing. Oog stopped as he was going down the stairs. 'She is very lovely, your Sara.'

Light from the large window showed the blush on Harry's cheeks.

'I hope you will soon be friends again,' said Oog.

Harry went back to his office. He sat a while in silence. The evening and the way Sara had helped throughout made him feel braver. She would not have done all she had if she didn't care for him. *Be brave* he thought. Harry took up his mobile and called Sara's number.

40

WITNESS STATEMENT

Statement of: *Agnes Leonard*
Age if under 18: *over 18*
Occupation: *Waitress at The Red Lion*

This statement (consisting of 1 page(s) each signed by me) is true to the best of my knowledge and belief and I make it knowing that, if it is tendered in evidence, I shall be liable to prosecution if I have wilfully stated in it anything which I know to be false, or do not believe to be true.
Witness Signature: *Agnes Leonard* Date: *07/12/2024*

I am still the abovenamed Agnes Leonard. The inspector has taken a second statement now that we know Tom Black is the killer. It's hard to believe. If I hadn't heard what went on in the Oak Room I wouldn't have believed it.

So I didn't say everything in my last statement but I always knew that it wasn't my cousin Paul who killed the dead woman. I did see him coming out of the bar when I was taking a tray back to the kitchen. I said Hi but he didn't notice. He was crying. Like who cries when they just done a murder? So I knew all the time it wasn't him. He was wiping his eyes, poor man and it made me feel so sad for him. What happened to upset him so much? Did that woman deserve to die? I need to know more of what went on. Was she playing Paul and Tom against each other?

I said it was the drunk man from the big group in my other statement. I didn't know if that was true but I had to stand up for my cousin. And where have they taken my cousin? I saw him in the back of a police car and that wife of his in another. They had to get more cars out from Ely. I happened to hear that by accident like.

I was so worried when I heard that Paul had fainted. And all the time the killer was Tom Black. What will my dad say when he hears? But the big thing is that my cousin did not kill that woman and I always said that.

---

* * * * *

WITNESS STATEMENT

Statement of: *Elsie Clay*
Age if under 18: *over 18* Occupation: *student and waitress*

This statement (consisting of 2 page(s) each signed by me) is true to the best of my knowledge and belief and I make it knowing that, if it is tendered in evidence, I shall be liable to prosecution if I have wilfully stated in it anything which I know to be false, or do not believe to be true.
Witness Signature: *Elsie Clay* Date: *07/12/2024*

I am the abovenamed person. I work part time at the Red

Lion. At weekends. I'm at college during the week.

I'm sorry I ran off and that the Inspector had to send a squad car to bring me back. I was so frightened because I saw the man who must have killed the woman. I was in the corridor. I had just delivered desserts to table 6. I saw a man standing outside the bar. He was very quiet but then I heard him growl. It frightened me, so I went into the kitchen but, well I was curious too. Should I say anything? But if I told Donna about it she might have said that I was being silly. I'd been in trouble earlier – not with Donna – it was Agnes, but anyway I didn't think I could say anything to Donna about Mr Black if I didn't have proof. And a growl could have meant anything.

I have nothing against Mr Black. Agnes says he's a regular and he does tip well.

I don't usually spy on people but I heard crying from the bar and Mr Black was just standing there and not helping the person crying. That was mean. So that's why I opened the kitchen door just a bit and watched.

I realised afterwards that it was actually Paul Leonard who was making the dead woman cry. But while I was watching, Mr Black suddenly dived into the disabled toilet. He didn't close the door. He left it slightly open. Then I saw Paul Leonard coming out of the bar. I know who he is because Agnes kept talking about him all evening. He's her cousin. He looked very upset. He stopped and wiped his eyes and nose before going back to the Oak Room. So he must have been the one to make the woman cry but he was upset too. And she was still crying after he left.

As soon as Paul Leonard was out of sight, Mr Black came out from the disabled toilet and went into the bar. I heard him being friendly to the woman. I thought that was nice, that he was going to comfort her.

I crept out of the kitchen and stood close to the wall.

He was saying to the woman that he could make her happy. It was hard to hear but I think she said no never.

Mr Black stopped when she said that. Instead of going over to her, he turned left to where the bar is. Then I saw him cross over to the right side of the bar.

I now know the woman was sitting on the sofa near to the fire exit. I heard him talking again and she said something I couldn't hear, but I did hear her gulp or something. I only had time to get back behind the door when Mr Black came out of the bar. He was moving quickly. I closed the kitchen door.

Mr Black must have gone into one of the toilets because Agnes came into the kitchen after me and she said she'd seen nothing. That surprised me because Agnes is a very nosey person. I heard her say afterwards that the woman was dead. How would she know that if she hadn't gone into the bar. I don't trust Agnes.

When I heard there had been an accident, I felt frightened. I don't know why I didn't tell Donna or Lucy or the Inspector what I saw. I'm sorry I ran away. I just needed to think. I told my mum when I got home. She said I had to go back and tell the police. She said she would come with me and I wanted her to but the policeman who came to collect me said I had to go back on my own.

We were getting ready to drive to the Red Lion when the policeman turned up.

It's a relief to tell you what I saw. I'm so sorry about the dead woman. I wish I'd done something. Donna says she was killed instantly and there's nothing I could have done to stop that. But Donna is kind and nice. I'm not sure Agnes will be so kind especially as her cousin was suspected at one point. I'm just so sorry I didn't do something.

41

Sunday morning was Sunday morning in the Red Lion. Lucy, Donna, Agnes, Elsie and Vi were bustling about preparing for the lunchtime service. Donna was chewing the end of a pen as she checked through the bookings list. 'Busy today,' she said.

'Yes,' replied Lucy, taking a tiny break from cooking.

'Yes,' said Vi, who was doing veg prep.

Elsie was loading glasses onto a tray. 'Where am I to work today, Donna?'

'I'd like you to take the Victorian Room please, Elsie. Will you be okay?'

'I'll be fine, thanks.'

'Why is everyone acting like nothing just happened?' Agnes stopped what she was doing and moved into the centre of the kitchen.

'Because we have a busy lunchtime coming up and we have to adjust and…' Donna swallowed.

'…get back to normal,' filled in Lucy. 'It's been horrible, but life, and lunch and later on, dinner, go on. And so must we.'

'You're all weird. How can you just forget what's happened?' Agnes hiccupped.

Elsie left off filling her tray and walked over to Agnes. 'Would you like a hug, Agnes?' She stretched out her arms.

'Mmm um yes.' Agnes took the hug.

Donna looked at Lucy, who stared back and they both turned to Vi who, calm as she always was, simply shook her head. Absolute quiet descended for a few moments, broken only by the muffled sound of Agnes sniffing.

'Th…thank you,' she said, disengaging herself from Elsie, who returned to filling her tray.

'I'll put these on the Vic Room tables now.'

'Thanks Elsie,' said Donna who was running the cold tap over a napkin.

Lucy and Vi carried on working. Agnes continued to stand in the middle of the room.

'Here, Agnes,' said Donna, passing the saturated napkin to her. 'Close your eyes and hold this against them for a minute or two. It will refresh and cool them.'

Agnes placed her hands over the napkin to keep it in place. 'But it's not normal,' she said. 'The Oak Room and the Vic Room are lovely and tidy and I know you cleaned the kitchen again this morning and the cleaner has been deep-cleaning everything and double-scrubbing the toilets – well not the disabled one because that's got an 'Out of Order' sign on it – but it's just so weird because the bar is out of bounds and the curtain is drawn to hide the police tape and we never put the screen back in the Function Room and now it's standing up in front of the bar, and what are people who want to have a drink before lunch to do? And what are we going to say to them?' Agnes took a much-needed gulp of air at the end of this speech.

'How do you know there's police tape behind the curtain?' asked Donna.

'Because I looked, didn't I?'

'I hope you didn't go in,' said Lucy. 'It's been sealed off by the Forensic people and they warned us not to contaminate it.'

'I didn't go in. I didn't touch anything. I'm just just…'

'Upset,' said Elsie who had returned with an empty tray.

'You got the door right!' Agnes grinned at Elsie.

'Yes, and I remembered where the napkins are too.'

'Well I hope everything other than the bar and the disabled toilet is back to normal, because I need to make up for lost tips. Christmas is coming and I have lots to buy. And since I'm serving in the Oak Room, I hope the six people sitting at Inspector Harry's table and the other six at my cousin Paul's table are going to be generous.' Agnes threw the wet napkin into the laundry basket. 'And what are we to say to people when they ask why the police were here last night and when they ask who the killer is, and—'

'Nothing,' said Donna. 'Okay? Say nothing. You can give the excuse that the police have said we're not to discuss the incident. Okay?'

'But it'll be on my mind.'

'Speaking of your mind,' said Lucy. 'Please remember that what you call "Harry's table" is actually Table 14, and the table for six at the end by the window is Table 10 and NOT your cousin Paul's table. Can you remember that, Agnes?'

Agnes opened her eyes wide, shrugged. 'Okay okay. Like calm down. We should all just calm down.' Agnes picked up her half-filled tray and sprinted through the Out door.

'Stop grinning, Donna,' said Lucy as she turned back to her work.

42

Harry got out of the taxi. He had decided against asking a colleague to give him a lift to Sara's house. He preferred to keep things low key and not alert her neighbours. He had always tried to be careful about that.

Standing in front of her terraced house, Harry felt nervous. A low miaow sounded from inside the house. Harry walked up to the door and knocked.

Sara opened the door wide when she saw him. Out shot Arabella. The cat surprised Harry by winding around his lower legs. Harry looked up at Sara and laughed. This was a welcome he hadn't expected.

'Come in, Harry.'

Sara closed the door, leaving the cat outside on the mat.

Printed in Dunstable, United Kingdom

77428365R00119